I saw no  I
checked the be   le
carpet and peeked under the bed.

Still no violin.

I was beginning to think that Aaron Levy had deliberately thwarted me by taking his violin with him or putting it in the safe—an ungentlemanly thing for him to do, given all the time and effort I was putting into finding it. I returned to the front room and was about to check the last remaining door—probably a connection to the neighboring suite—when I almost tripped over something sticking out from under the sofa. I reached down to shove it back out of the way.

The violin.

How could someone treat an instrument so valuable in such a cavalier manner? More and more it seemed as if Mr. Aaron Levy was entirely too careless and had to be relieved of this heavy responsibility before someone…well…stole the damn thing!

And I was just the woman to do it. I opened the case and lifted up my trophy, held my flashlight close to it, and with great satisfaction, began to examine it lovingly.

And that's when the lights came on.

Murder with Strings Attached

by

Mark Reutlinger

Murder with Strings Attached

Cover Art by *Jennifer Greeff*

The Wild Rose Press, Inc.
PO Box 708
Adams Basin, NY 14410-0708
Visit us at www.thewildrosepress.com

Publishing History
First Crimson Rose Edition, 2021
Trade Paperback ISBN 978-1-5092-3321-2
Digital ISBN 978-1-5092-3322-9

Published in the United States of America

Dedication

To Analee and Elliot, and all the horses

"The older the violin, the sweeter the music."

~Larry McMurtry

Chapter 1

It was pitch dark in Aaron Levy's closet.

But then, that's the way most closets are, I suppose.

It was crowded. It was hot. It was stuffy. I was getting a cramp in my legs from crouching, and I was trying desperately to suppress a sneeze. Fair to say I was totally reassessing this entire enterprise.

Finally the suite door closed and I could assume I was alone. Slowly I opened the closet door and peeked out.

No one seemed to be there. I stepped out.

But of course I haven't yet explained what I was doing hiding in the closet of a famous violinist in the first place, have I? Or how a fairly simple case of burglary turned into a not-so-simple case of murder.

So perhaps I should begin at the beginning.

****

As you've gathered, I'm a burglar. Florence Palmer, second-story woman extraordinaire (or so I'd like to think), but you can call me Flo—everyone else does.

Of course, I wasn't always a burglar. Long story short, I couldn't afford college and took a job as a house cleaner to put myself through. Maybe that was a mistake, because being exposed to all those beautiful and obscenely expensive *tchotchkes*, all of which my clients could easily do without, wore me down. So one day I decided I was tired of dusting, and drooling over, other people's treasures. If I wasn't born with a silver spoon in my mouth, I'd just have to borrow someone else's.

But getting back to the story, I learned from a friend of mine—a woman named Janice Bailey, to be exact—who's a housekeeper at the posh Regency Hotel here in Seattle, that Aaron Levy was staying there in one of the fancy-shmancy suites. Yes, I mean *the* Aaron Levy, the renowned concert violinist. Anyway, she told me that, while cleaning his suite—the Royal Suite, no less—she came across Levy's violin case, stacked up with his luggage in his closet. She peeked inside, and there was his violin, just lying there. "It must be a Stradivarius," she said, "'cause isn't that what all the famous violinists play?" Sounded right to me.

"But surely he doesn't really keep a priceless violin in his hotel closet," I said. "That'd be pretty stupid."

"I suppose so," Janet said. "Anyway, I took a picture of it for my nephew. He's taking lessons. Here, I'll show you." She took out her phone and, after a bit of searching, found the picture and showed it to me.

Nice looking violin, but they all look alike to me. So I took out my own phone and found a picture of Aaron Levy's violin online, in a biographical article. I compared the two pictures.

They were identical, to every detail.

But it's not a Stradivarius, like we assumed it was. It's something called a Guarneri, which apparently is just as valuable.

And that's when I got my great idea, and how I ended up in that closet. I decided this was too good an opportunity to pass up. I mean, how often does an ordinary (if extremely talented) burglar get a chance to score a multi-million dollar prize?

Not bloody often.

****

I talked the idea over with my best friend, Sara Mandel. Sara's the only person who knows what I do for a living. She doesn't participate in my little escapades, but she's a good listener and is always ready to give me her opinion of my hare-brained schemes. So I told her about the priceless violin, just sitting there waiting for me. She thought I was crazy, of course.

"What would you do with it if you did get hold of it?" she asked. "It'd be too hot to sell, and last I checked, you don't play the violin."

"I wouldn't try to sell it," I said. "I wouldn't have a clue how or where to find a buyer for something that valuable. And that hot. No, what I'd do is ransom it back to Levy, for a reasonable price, of course. Enough to make the job worthwhile, but too little for him to resist very strenuously, given how wealthy he must be and that he really needs it for his performances.

"Besides, I'd be doing Levy a favor."

"How so?"

"You can see how careless he is with that violin. It would be in much safer hands if the hands it was in were mine. And as an added benefit, he'd learn to take much better care of it—like keeping it in the hotel safe—in the future, don't you think?"

Sara had to agree, although reluctantly. "Sure," she said. "Makes you a genuine good Samaritan."

I hate it when she gets sarcastic like that.

****

I did a little more research on Guarneri violins, then reported back to Sara.

"Turns out some concert violinists consider Guarneris to be superior to Stradivariuses—no wait, that isn't right, is it? Superior to Stadivarii, I think it is."

"Whatever. My Italian's a little rusty. So who was this Guarneri?"

"Actually, there were several famous instrument makers in the Guarneri family, but the greatest was…" (I consulted my notes) "Bartolomeo Giuseppe Guarneri del Gesu."

"That's a mouthful."

"It is, isn't it? That Guarneri not only made Aaron Levy's violin, he also made those of other famous violinists like Heifetz and Paganini. Paganini's, it seems, was nicknamed 'The Cannon'; must've had a helluva sound. Anyway, I learned that the way to tell if it's the genuine article, other than how it looks, is by its label."

"Violins have labels?"

"Apparently these do, on the inside. The labels on Del Gesu violins incorporate the Greek abbreviation for Jesus, I.H.S., and a cross, because Del Gesu means 'of Jesus.' And the most exciting thing is that because he died young, Giuseppe created only 174 violins, far fewer than Mr. Stradivari, and they can fetch—are you ready?—ten million dollars or more at auction." I broke into a sweat just repeating that.

And from the way her mouth fell open when I said it, I think Sara was pretty impressed too.

****

We adjourned to my computer. I recalled seeing an article about Levy in the Seattle Times. "Here it is," I

4

said, with Sara looking over my shoulder. "Let's see: Born in Tel Aviv, graduated from Julliard, lives in New York. Started playing the violin at five years old, something of a prodigy. Now he travels all over the world performing....And here's his schedule." I checked the dates.

"Damn! Gonna be in town for only about a week. He's performing twice in Seattle—Tuesday and Thursday—and once down in Tacoma, on Friday. He's also giving a radio interview on an FM station on Wednesday morning. "

"So when do you think it'd be best to do this?" Sara asked. "Looks like Wednesday and Friday are the best bets."

"I think Wednesday," I said after thinking it over. "We can be sure he'll be out of his suite in the morning, and not sleeping in."

"You'll have to act pretty fast—tomorrow's already Monday," Sara said, stating the obvious. But she was right. I had no time to lose.

I decided the best way to get into Levy's suite was by pretending to be what I once was—a cleaner, or in this case a hotel maid, like Janice. I'd have to do it on Janice's day off, of course, so I didn't run into her somewhere in the hotel and have to explain what I was doing there in her uniform. But there I was lucky, because I knew Janice was off until Thursday.

Monday morning I phoned local uniform supply companies until I found the one that supplies the Regency. I told them I was hired as a temp and needed to rent a uniform. No problem—they even had my size. I zipped downtown and picked it up.

I then decided I needed to make a "dry run," to get

the lay of the land, before Wednesday. On Tuesday I would don the new uniform and head for the Regency Hotel for a little reconnaissance.

I was excited. Operation Violin was about to begin.

Chapter 2

The next morning, Tuesday, my alarm clock went off at seven, not a time familiar to me since I adopted a mostly nocturnal profession. I batted the offending clock into submission and reluctantly slid out of bed. I took a quick shower, found my way into some underwear, slipped on my newly acquired uniform, and put my hair up in a ponytail. Looking somewhat respectable, I headed for the Regency.

The Regency Hotel is one of the venerable survivors of many layers of urban renewal, exhibiting a turn-of-the-century style that has been updated only as necessary for the comfort and convenience of its guests. It's not to my taste, but its art deco design and its stubborn embrace of the early Twentieth Century gives it a certain cache that appeals to celebrities and to anyone who is tired of sheer glass walls and severe minimalist architecture. And who has a pile of money. In any event, I was not there to critique, but to work. I first had to find out how to get onto the Concierge Level, where the Royal Suite was located, and which I suspected would not be accessible to just any riff-raff.

I entered the hotel wearing over my uniform a long, threadbare coat that had once been French blue, which I'd purchased at the Salvation Army thrift store for three dollars. I ignored the disdainful look I and my coat received from the liveried doorman. Fortunately, he was not charged with preventing citizens from entering on the basis of their attire, although he looked as if he wished he were.

My first destination was the Ladies' Lounge, which I found by following a sign that pointed down a flight of stairs to the lower level. There I got my first real taste of the Regency's ambiance: marble floors, stalls and counters; gold-plated fixtures; and art deco sconces casting soft light around large, oval mirrors. I entered one of the stalls and hung my coat on the elegant cast-brass coat hook. It looked totally out of place, like a hobo sitting on a throne. And speaking of thrones, I took the opportunity to use the toilet—who knew when I'd have another chance—then stepped out of the stall, leaving the coat inside to be picked up later. If it was still there, that is. If it was gone, I was out three bucks.

I was finally ready for action.

The lobby of the Regency follows the hotel's theme of nostalgic elegance. Its ceiling is high, and from it hang several massive crystal and gold chandeliers. The front desk is of polished marble, with the obligatory computers and other electronic aids discreetly concealed. My destination was the bank of elevators just across from the front desk. There are three elevators, and although they have the appearance of having been installed when the hotel was built, complete with a mechanical pointer over each to indicate the floor it's on, the hotel has long since updated the mechanisms and retired its human elevator operators in favor of self-service buttons. The buttons cannot make small talk or direct one to the hotel café, but neither do they require a salary, an eight-hour workday, or health benefits.

I pushed the ornate button marked "up," and within a few seconds the doors of the center elevator opened. Armed only with my uniform and a small duster I had brought for effect, I took a deep breath and marched into the elevator as if I knew where I was going. Inside it was as plush as the lobby itself, if not more so, with rich walnut paneling, inlaid rosewood trim, and polished brass rails. I had seen pictures of the interiors of the luxury rail cars on the Orient Express that were less imposing. Turning, I glanced at the brass-framed console. The display revealed that floors one through eight could be reached simply by pressing the appropriate button, but floor nine, labeled "Concierge Level," required an extra step. In the old days, that step probably would have been to show one's room key to the operator. In the electronic age, those guests with rooms on that hallowed level have to swipe their magnetic room key through a card reader before they can direct it to floor nine. I assumed employees could do the same using a universal key card of some sort. I, of course, didn't have a key card and had little prospect of acquiring one in the next few minutes.

Following behind me onto the elevator was an older gentleman who reeked of cigar smoke. *At least in the case of cigars*, I said to myself, *smokers as well as smoking should be banned from elevators*. I almost wished he were still smoking the horrid thing; at least then I could, with righteous indignation, tell him to put it out or get out. It was more problematic to insist he take off his clothes. Instead, I stepped off the elevator just before the doors closed. Let him reek alone.

****

Back in the lobby, I continued my survey of access

points. Around a corner from the front desk I spied what appeared to be a service elevator. As I approached, its identity was confirmed by a sign printed in black on the wide gray door reading "Employees only." Apparently employees could call the service elevator by punching a code into a keypad where the "up" and "down" buttons would ordinarily reside.

Given, then, the two possible ways to reach the Concierge Level, my choice was easy: I would have to learn the secret code of the service elevator.

I considered several possible ways of obtaining the magic numbers, from bribing one of the housekeepers, which I dismissed as too risky, to seducing one of the bellhops, which I dismissed as lunacy. I finally settled on the tried and true method by which safe combinations, and more recently credit card and PIN numbers, have been obtained over the years: close observation. I would have to hang around the elevator long enough, and see the code punched in often enough, to learn the sequence.

It took me three separate five-minute sessions dusting the display cases adjacent to the service elevator, as various employees came along and punched in their codes, before I had worked out the four-key cipher. Twice I had to abandon my post when passing manager-types eyed me quizzically, returning only when the coast was again clear.

By fitting those five-minute sessions into a 45-minute time frame, I eventually had the numbers I needed. Finally, I checked out possible escape routes, including the fire stairs inside and the fire escape outside. The management could make the Concierge floor as difficult to enter as they liked; but the Fire

Marshal would be greatly offended were there to be any difficulty in leaving it in an emergency. And I could think of no greater emergency than hot pursuit by the authorities.

Having completed my reconnaissance mission, I returned to the Ladies' Lounge to retrieve my coat, on the chance it was still there. I was actually very pleased—and a bit surprised—to see that it was. It apparently had encountered no thieves to steal it, no good Samaritans to turn it in, just ordinary folks content to leave well enough (and faded old coats) alone. Just as well, because I still had one more use for my thrift shop treasure.

Tomorrow, when Operation Violin began for real.

Chapter 3

Wednesday. Showtime!

I again left my coat in the Ladies' Lounge and of course used the toilet. Having to pee in the middle of a job can only lead to trouble of one kind or another. Passing the front desk on my way to the elevator, I wanted to avoid eye contact with any of the clerks on duty. But, like Lot's wife, I couldn't resist just a peek. Unfortunately, one of the check-in clerks, an older woman with gray hair pulled back into a tight bun, happened to be looking in my direction and our eyes met.

The woman immediately called to me, "Miss, would you please step over here?"

I returned a mimed "Who, me?" gesture. The bun lady nodded in the affirmative.

I just had to look, didn't I? But I knew I now had no choice but to comply. I walked over slowly as I tried frantically to think of answers, having no idea what the questions might be. Would I be asked who I was and what I was doing here? If so, would my answers be credible? When I reached the desk I tried to act nonchalant.

"Yes, ma'am?"

The bun lady said, "Just a moment, please," and reached under the desk.

Totally irrationally it flashed through my mind that

the woman was going to pull out a pistol and place me under arrest. Good thing I'd just peed, or I'd probably have done it now. It's amazing what tricks a guilty conscience can play on you. What she actually pulled out, however, was a stack of letters. She handed them to me and, motioning toward a mail box mounted on the far wall, said, "Would you be a dear and drop these in the box over there?"

I accepted the letters and the assignment with relief. "Certainly, ma'am. No problem."

I marched directly over to the mail box and deposited the letters. I then continued on my way to the service elevator, this time resisting any urge to look anywhere but straight ahead.

I hoped to ride up to the Concierge Level alone, to avoid any further awkward moments with real employees. To my chagrin, however, no sooner had I punched in the code I had purloined the previous day than a fresh-faced young man, wearing a conservative gray suit and burgundy red tie, drew up beside me. His badge identified him as Larry Avery, an assistant manager. He said nothing, but just waited, smiling at me when I glanced sideways to size him up. When the elevator did not come, both I and Assistant Manager Avery began to fidget, me with my duster and he by rocking slightly back and forth on his heels, hands clasped behind him. We looked at each other; he smiled again.

Suddenly it occurred to me that the reason the elevator was not coming was that either I had pressed a wrong button when putting in the code or somehow the code had been changed since yesterday. *Geez, who are they afraid is going to use the damn elevator?* But of course I was in fact the very type of person they were afraid might use it, as I well knew.

I turned and smiled at Larry. "I must have pressed a wrong key," I said in my most innocent and ingenuous voice—a good trick when over 40 and far from being either. I resisted batting my eyelashes or giggling and adding, "Silly me."

As I had anticipated, Larry, being a gentleman—and more to the point being a man in a position to aid a somewhat attractive lady—stepped over to the key pad and gallantly punched in the current code. More smiles. Good old Larry.

I watched carefully and memorized the new code as best I could. "Thanks," I said.

Smile and nod from Larry.

The elevator arrived as requested, and Larry stepped aside to let me enter. The cab was twice as big as the guest elevator I had ridden the day before, and instead of polished walnut it was lined with metal "diamond plate" sheets protected all around with painted wooden rails. I was followed in by Larry, and behind him trundled a room service cart, pushed by a waiter wearing a white apron, with the most delicious aromas—I guessed bacon, eggs, and waffles—wafting from under two elegant silver plate covers. The waiter maneuvered his cart toward the back of the car, parking it next to me. The contrast in bouquet with the stinky cigar odor of the previous day's elevator ride was extreme. But pleasant as was the aroma, it reminded me that I had had no more than a cup of coffee as I rushed out of my apartment that morning, and it was all I could do to keep from surreptitiously snatching the bran muffin sitting on a plate next to me. But I could hardly risk blowing my cover, not to mention being arrested for muffin theft, when there was so much more at stake. Other than the rumbling of my stomach, I suffered in silence.

The doors closed and Assistant Manager Larry stepped over to the console. *Please don't be going to the Concierge Level.* I was greatly relieved when he pressed "8," then turned to ask for my floor. "Nine, please," I replied shyly, and he duly pressed the corresponding button. He made the same inquiry of the waiter, who fortunately was going only to the second floor with his aromatic breakfast banquet.

The service elevator's progress was much slower and noisier than that of the guest lifts, perhaps because of its hard surfaces and the heavier loads it was meant to carry. After what seemed like minutes (it was actually about 20 seconds) the display above the console flashed "2," the noise and motion stopped, the doors rattled open, and the waiter and his cart, bran muffin and all, backed out of the elevator. The doors closed, the elevator resumed its creep upwards, and the assistant manager and I were alone.

I hoped Larry would skip the strained small talk so common when only two people share an elevator ride. My hopes were dashed, however, before we had reached the next floor.

"I don't recall seeing you around before," he said with a cheerful smile.

"No, I'm a replacement for one of the girls who called in sick."

"Oh, I see. Who was that?"

Geez, can't this thing go any faster? I smiled and said, "I'm sorry, they didn't tell me that. Just that I was

15

needed for the day."

"Well, welcome to the Regency," Larry said magnanimously, as if he were the owner and not a hired flunky like me. "Let me know if you have any questions about anything."

"Why, thank you, sir. I certainly will." This time I suppressed the urge to curtsy.

Larry got out at the eighth floor, with another smile and a nod. I smiled and nodded back. The door closed. Then I finally exhaled.

****

At nine, the Concierge Level, I straightened my skirt, hitched up my bra, and adjusted my duster as I stepped off the elevator, hoping I looked as if I belonged there. It was 9:50 a.m.

Although I had intended to arrive a few minutes before the cleaning staff, I saw that in fact I was late, or at best just in time. All the maids were already busy in the rooms, as evidenced by the cleaning carts parked outside of three rooms with their doors open. And yes, one of those rooms, the second from the elevator, had a plaque outside that proclaimed it to be the "Royal Suite." Target sighted; prepare to attack.

My plan required the door to be open and the maid to be busy somewhere she could not see the front room, preferably cleaning the bathroom. Then I could slip into the Royal Suite undetected, hide in a closet or other suitable place, wait until the maid left, then search for the violin. I knew it was the "undetected" part that could prove tricky.

Acting as casual as I could, I sauntered past the door of the Royal Suite, duster dusting, and as I passed the open door, I peeked inside. There was the maid—

the real maid—apparently beginning to straighten the front room, which did not look like it needed much straightening. The maid glanced up just as I was passing, our eyes briefly met, and I was certain the woman would say something…awkward. But she only smiled and returned to her duties. *Maybe she's new here too.*

Did you ever try to hang around a place where no one is supposed to be hanging around at all, looking innocent and inconspicuous, when you pretty clearly were neither? I adjusted my uniform, pretended to look for something I dropped on the carpet, and generally tried to be invisible. It wasn't easy.

During the ten minutes or so it took the maid to finish cleaning the living room of the Royal Suite, the only dangerous person I encountered was one of the guests, a young, elegantly-dressed blonde woman, who came out of a room down the hall and walked past me to the elevator. After pressing the "down" button, she turned toward me. I was still on my hands and knees pretending to look for the nonexistent bauble I dropped, deliberately facing away from the intruder, trying to ignore her. Just as the elevator was arriving, the woman said, "You, down there!" I looked up. "When you clean Room 914, make sure you empty all the wastebaskets this time. I don't want to find one of them still full, like yesterday. Understand?"

My mouth dropped open. I was speechless, both because I had nothing useful (or civil) to say, and because before I could think of an appropriately cutting response, the elevator door was already closing behind the silly bitch. Just as well.

Returning my attention to the Royal Suite, I peeked

in the door and saw that the maid had picked up her portable carrier containing cleaning supplies and was heading into the bathroom. I hurriedly got to my feet. As soon as I heard the bathroom water running, after checking to see there was no one else in the hallway at that moment, I darted into the suite, glanced around, spotted a closet, and as quietly as possible opened the door, entered, and closed the door behind me.

And there, as the maid dutifully sanitized the bathroom and then tidied up the separate bedroom, I sat, and sat, for almost an hour. Or rather squatted some, sat on the floor some, stood some. Despite the relative luxury of the suite's appointments, the management had neglected to provide its guests with a chair or other suitable place to sit in their closet.

Finally the maid left the suite, taking her cleaning supplies and her sweet time, closing the door behind her, and I was finally alone.

And I believe this is where you came in.

****

I silently exhaled and opened the door of the closet a bit. I peeked out, and finding the coast indeed to be clear, stepped out.

The hunt was on.

From Janice's description, the violin should have been in the closet, but I had been in the closet for quite a while, and so far as I could tell, I had not been accompanied in there by a violin. But it had been hard to search carefully without light and the risk of making noise, so now I opened the closet door again and checked more carefully, using my flashlight.

No violin.

I looked around the room, which was almost as

dark as the closet. Although it was a bright day, the real maid had closed the heavy red-and-gold tapestry drapes that were covering the full-wall windows, letting in almost no light. I didn't want to risk turning on the lamps or the chandelier, casting light that might be noticed under the door from the hallway, so I still had to rely on my small flashlight to make my inspection of the premises. Waving it around to get my bearings, I could see that the fancy chandelier that hung from the ceiling was comparable in elegance to those hanging in the lobby, but on a smaller scale. Even in the limited light, its crystal bangles twinkled and sparkled expensively. Unfortunately, it was too big to take away with me.

The rest of the room's décor was similarly opulent. The coffee table, either antique French provincial or a good imitation thereof, was painted in a light cream color, as was the large credenza against the far wall, probably filled with complimentary drinks and snacks. Two overstuffed chairs were upholstered in the same pattern as the drapes. The walls were covered in an old-fashioned floral-patterned wallpaper, with the carved-wood moldings painted to match the furnishings. I aimed my flashlight on all the room's surfaces, looking for my prize.

Alas, no violin.

I tried the doors on the far wall. The bathroom provided no place for a violin to hide. Behind another door was a bedroom, in which a four-poster bed resided. It was covered by an elegant canopy of red and gold tapestry that matched the drapes and chairs. A highboy and a vanity table completed the bedroom furnishings. I saw nothing interesting in plain sight, so I checked the bedroom closet and then lay flat on the carpet and peeked under the bed.

Still no violin.

I was beginning to think that Aaron Levy had deliberately thwarted me by taking his violin with him or putting it in the safe—an ungentlemanly thing for him to do, given all the time and effort I was putting into finding it. I returned to the front room and was about to check the last remaining door—probably a connection to the neighboring suite—when I almost tripped over something sticking out from under the sofa. I reached down to shove it back out of the way.

The violin.

How could someone treat an instrument so valuable in such a cavalier manner? More and more it seemed as if Mr. Aaron Levy was entirely too careless and had to be relieved of this heavy responsibility before someone…well…stole the damn thing!

And I was just the woman to do it. I opened the case and lifted up my trophy, held my flashlight close to it, and with great satisfaction, began to examine it lovingly.

And that's when the lights came on.

Chapter 4

"It's a fake!"

The words were spoken simultaneously by me, as I was staring down at the now-fully-illuminated violin in my hand—a beautiful violin, but missing that all-important Guarneri label—and by a smiling man of medium height and build standing in the doorway with his hand on the light switch, presumably the rightful owner of said violin.

Our two voices probably could not have achieved a more harmonious duet if we had rehearsed for weeks; despite the unfortunate blend of Aaron Levy's raspy baritone with my unsteady contralto, it was not too badly out of tune.

For several seconds we simply stared at each other: the discoverer and the discoveree; the violated and the violator. Then, just when the tension seemed to be building to a peak, we both began to laugh. Although that is not a usual result of the owner of valuable property surprising a burglar in the act of stealing it, clearly neither of us perceived the other as a threat, and I guess we both appreciated the comic irony of the situation. But still neither of us was inclined to begin a conversation.

Well, someone has to break the ice. Although I couldn't recall whether Emily Post had anything specific to say about this particular social occasion, I decided that, as the uninvited guest, it was my place to go first.

"You know," I began, a bit more breezily than I felt, "generally it isn't considered polite to disturb a woman in a…um…an intimate activity."

The man in the doorway—for he still had only one foot in the room and his hand on the doorknob—smiled and said, "I suppose I could come back later. But it will still be a fake. Or more precisely, a copy." I thought he had a nice smile.

"Yes, I suppose so." I looked sadly at the ersatz Guarneri. At least I wouldn't be making a very embarrassing attempt to hold for a king's ransom a violin hardly worth the ransom of a poor vassal. On the other hand, Aaron Levy's untimely entrance might mean my very first trip to the pokey, which I definitely did not relish.

"But why," I asked, "do you keep a fake Guarneri in your room, when you own the real thing? Just to toy with people like me?" I guess I almost sounded indignant. In a way, I was.

"Whoa," the violinist responded, stepping into the room and closing the door, "it wasn't my idea to have you break into my room and try to steal my violin. I think you'll have to take some responsibility for that." Fortunately, he was still smiling.

"Oh, I do," I hastened to assure him, meanwhile turning off my flashlight and putting it in my pocket. "It was all my idea. But just the same, if you hadn't put this imitation in such a vulnerable place and tempted people like me—well, me anyway—I wouldn't be standing here like a damn fool facing a long stretch in Alcatraz."

Levy began to laugh again, but he quickly controlled himself. "First of all," he said, "I think they closed Alcatraz, at least as a prison, several years ago. And second, who said you were going to prison?"

"Well, no one," I admitted, "but I guess that's the usual result when, as I believe they say in court, the lawful owner of valuable property comes upon a burglar attempting to dispossess him of said property."

Now Levy did start to laugh. He sat down in one of the suite's overstuffed chairs, softly cushioned and fitted with carved wooden feet, and he gestured for me to do the same. I reluctantly complied and sat in the matching chair, not sure what this strange musician was up to. I lowered myself cautiously into the billowy sea of a down-filled cushion, immediately sinking what felt like several feet into its depths. I wondered whether I would be able to get out without assistance.

Apparently what seemed like a straightforward case of caught-in-the-act to me was more complex, or at least more nuanced, to Levy. He appeared to be thinking the entire situation through. Finally he said, "The way I see it, when I found you, you were contemplating 'dispossessing' me, to use your fancy term, of what was in fact a relatively valueless piece of property, at least by Stradivarius or Guarneri standards. But as I interrupted you before you could carry out your nefarious intention, the most I could accuse you of would be unworthy thoughts and grandiose plans. And how often do our grandiose plans fail to come to fruition?"

He paused to consider this philosophical query, giving me time to do the same. "And of course there is the fact that you snuck into my room without my knowledge—I assume you're not a real chambermaid, am I correct?"

I acknowledged as much with a nod of my head and an appropriately contrite expression.

"As I thought. But seeing as how I don't really live here, and God-knows-how-many strangers come in and out during the day without my knowledge, to vacuum the carpet, fix the air conditioner, or leave those awful little chocolates on the bed, why should I be concerned if you come in to do a little unworthy contemplation?"

I didn't know quite how to respond to this brilliant exculpatory argument, which I felt was worthy of a very good defense attorney. But before I could say anything, Levy added, "And while I mention it, just how did you get into my room? I don't see any evidence of forced entry—broken locks, jimmied windows, that sort of thing."

At least I was now on firmer ground. "Oh, that. I just found out when your room would be cleaned, rented a uniform, learned the code for the service elevator, hung around looking like I belonged until the real maid was busy in the bathroom, and snuck into the closet until she left." I omitted the part about my friend Janice's inadvertent assistance, not wanting to take a chance that he would pass that information along to the management. One must always protect one's sources, including unintentional sources.

Levy thought about that for a minute, then asked me, "Are you usually this clever in getting into places you want to…to get into?"

"Well," I said, "I don't like to brag or anything, but I don't think there are too many places I couldn't find some way into; and those I couldn't, I'm probably better off staying out of."

"Hmm…a pretty sound philosophy," Levy said, rubbing his chin.

But I wanted to return the conversation, which had drifted off toward hypothetical unlawful entries in the abstract, back to the actual unlawful entry at hand. "So, taking into account your excellent summation of my situation a minute ago, just what do you plan to do with me, now that you've caught me?"

Levy looked directly at me, so that I felt a little chill go down my back. *This must be what a rainbow trout feels like when it's just been landed.* I was hoping Levy practiced catch and release. But the violinist seemed to be giving my question considerable thought. Either that or he was giving my long hair and short skirt considerable scrutiny. Or maybe both. Never underestimate the value of a good figure.

Finally he said, almost wistfully, "Nothing. You're free to leave. Like they say in basketball, 'no harm, no foul'."

Having played basketball myself, I was very familiar with that phrase, and I wasted no time in putting it to the test. "That's really very kind of you," I said in as sincere a tone as I could muster. "It's very generous of you to…to let me off the hook like this." That trout analogy seemed to be stuck in my head. I had an urge to give Levy a hug but decided that would be inappropriate.

I rose to leave, which as I mentioned took some effort, again thanked Mr. Levy for his understanding, and made my way to the suite's door, much relieved. But just as I was about to pass over the threshold to freedom, Levy called out, "No, wait!"

For a second I considered making a run for it, but that seemed out of keeping with the civilized way in which the matter had been handled up to this point, so I quickly rejected that impulse and stopped midway through the door.

Levy was still sitting in his overstuffed chair and seemed to be thinking very hard about something. He gestured with his hand, palm outward, that I should wait until he could think through whatever it was.

I waited. It wasn't easy.

After probably two minutes, during which I perspired more than I had during the entire operation up until then, Levy looked up at me and asked, "Do you think it's possible that you might be willing to do a little, uh, something for me?" Then he added, before I could reply, "Well, maybe not so little."

Completely taken aback by this turn in the conversation, I could only reply with the obvious question, "What did you have in mind?"

Levy now seemed to relax a bit. He stood up and gestured me back into the room, walking over and closing the door behind me. I wondered whether what he had in mind had sexual overtones, requiring me to earn my freedom with my body; but somehow I didn't get the kind of vibrations from him that I generally did when someone was about to hit on me, or to suggest I do something my parents wouldn't have approved of. (Of course, they wouldn't have approved of burglary either, but I had long ago come to terms with that small failure to meet my parents' expectations.) Mind you, I have nothing against a roll in the hay with a rich celebrity; I just don't want to have to buy my freedom with it. So I went back to the billowy sea of down, sank back below the surface, and waited for Mr. Levy's proposition.

"First," he began, "now that we're no longer burdened with the…uh…little contretemps of the last few minutes, I think we should properly introduce ourselves and start over on a more business-like basis."

Then, before I could answer, Levy rose from his chair and said, apologetically, "I'm sorry—I guess I should offer you a drink first. You've had a pretty rough day so far."

I couldn't agree more with that sentiment, and I definitely could use a drink. My host and erstwhile victim went over to the credenza, which as I had suspected contained a mini bar/liquor cabinet. I could see an assortment of little bottles with fancy labels, plus the usual soft drinks, salty snacks, and candy bars. Levy opened two little bottles, poured the brown liquid from each into a glass taken from a shelf above the credenza, and returned with them to the sitting area. He handed one of the drinks to me, and I accepted with thanks.

"To greater success—with someone else's possessions, of course—in the future," toasted Levy, and he and I drank to that.

"Now," Levy continued, "I assume you already know who I am. But just in case you have me confused with some other world-famous fiddler, I'm Aaron Levy. You can call me Aaron—all my closest friends and burglars do. So now I'm at a disadvantage."

I was feeling quite relaxed in the warmth of this gregarious virtuoso's considerable charm and enthusiasm, not to mention the warmth of my straight bourbon. I answered, "My name's Florence Palmer, but everyone calls me Flo."

"It's a pleasure to meet you, Flo," Aaron responded, sounding as if he meant it, "even if the circumstances are a bit…a bit awkward. And is this sort of thing" —he gestured toward the Guarneri-like instrument— "what you do for a living?"

"I'm afraid it is. I tried several other professions— all of them on the right side of the law, I might say— before I found the one that offered the kind of challenges and rewards that I was looking for."

"I see. And are you pretty good at it, today's little hitch notwithstanding?"

"Well, I certainly had thought so. Even today, I had every reason to believe that you kept a real Guarneri in your room, and that you would be tied up in some kind of interview for most of the afternoon. The cleaners had just left, so I should have had at least a half hour to myself. Just goes to show you that the best laid plans…."

Before Aaron could respond, I added, "But I still want to know what a fake violin is doing in your room. Why's it here?"

"Hey, you can never have too many violins," Aaron said with a slight smile.

"And where's the real one?"

Aaron, now no longer smiling and somewhat troubled, stood up and began to pace the floor. He turned to me and said, "Yes, where indeed. That's exactly what I want to talk to you about."

Chapter 5

Aaron Levy returned to his chair and turned to face me, while I, still not entirely sure what to make of the last several minutes, sat forward and waited for him to begin.

I took notice for the first time of Aaron's appearance, having thus far been totally focused on my awkward predicament. Aaron was about my middle-forties age, somewhat stocky build, with almost-black hair cut a bit long—*probably so he can toss it dramatically while he plays*, I thought. He was wearing an expensive-looking sport coat and slacks with a jaunty multi-color tie. Although not appearing overweight, he probably could stand to shed a few extra pounds, doubtless the result of long hours practicing the violin rather than working out at the gym. He had cherubic features and a nonthreatening demeanor, with a warm smile that seemed to be just beneath even his sternest look. *Seems like a nice guy.*

"First, let me explain about the violin," Aaron said. "I had a few weeks to myself before this gig in Seattle, so I thought I'd arrive early and do some sightseeing and maybe relax a bit, which I don't often have time to do."

"Too busy practicing, I assume."

"Mostly that. Anyway, I drove here in a rented car from L.A., where I'd been performing. The very day I got here, my Guarneri—the real one, I mean—was stolen from my car."

"You mean you left a priceless violin in a car? All by itself?" I was incredulous.

"Yeah, I don't believe it myself. It was really stupid. I was traveling alone, and I stopped at a rest stop and ran into the restroom for…well, for just a minute or two."

"And that was enough?"

"It was. Apparently I was being followed. Someone was just waiting for an opportunity, and I handed it to them."

"I assume you called the police?"

"Well, no. You'll see why in a moment. I assumed that, following a well-known pattern, the thief would soon contact me and ask for some kind of ransom to recover the violin. Then I could go to the police and maybe set some kind of trap for him."

Since this was just what I had intended to do, I wondered whether I would have fallen into such a trap.

Of course I would.

"This has happened to you before?" I asked.

"No, but it has to other artists I know. Anyway, I waited a few days but heard nothing. I was getting worried that maybe the violin was stolen by some damn amateur who would try to hock it for a few dollars, or accidentally damage it, and I might never get it back. You can't trust high-class merchandise to a low-class thief."

"I can see your point," I agreed. As I considered myself to be in the upper tier among burglars, I didn't take offense.

"I was about to go to the police, hoping they could

search pawn shops and other places it might end up, when I got a call from someone I used to know, someone I helped out financially when he was in trouble some years ago. He now works for James Edward Sanders."

"Isn't he a billionaire oil baron or something?" I asked.

"Not exactly. Billionaire yes, or at least many tens of millions. But he made his money in the grocery business—mega-supermarkets and all that."

"Sorry to interrupt. Go on."

"Right. So I got this call, from my friend. His name's Rafael, by the way. He wanted to return the favor. He told me that while working at Sanders' home, he had learned, quite by accident—he overheard a conversation he wasn't supposed to hear—that Sanders was the one who stole my violin. Or rather had it stolen. Obviously, he wouldn't go out and steal it himself."

"Probably not," I agreed. "But why would someone that rich steal anything, especially your violin?"

"Remember, it's not just any violin. That particular violin has been owned by some of the most famous violinists in history—myself included, I am immodest enough to say." He had the grace to smile a bit sheepishly. "In other words, it's one of a kind, and any collector would kill to add it to his collection. Or at least some collectors would steal to get it."

"So this Sanders guy is a violin collector and stole it for his collection?"

"I wish it were that simple," Aaron said sadly. "But it's a bit more complicated."

"How so?"

"Well, it seems, according to Rafael, Sanders is a

collector, but not particularly of violins. While he has some rare instruments, he collects mostly art, and especially paintings, Monet and other French impressionists to be specific. Has one of the largest private collections of Monet's paintings in the world. Some he's displayed publicly, at his home, or lent to various museums for exhibits."

I was getting confused. "I think I lost you there. What have Monet paintings to do with Guarneri violins?"

"I'm coming to that. It's generally suspected in the collector community that Sanders, like certain other wealthy art collectors in the world, has both his 'public' collection, which the world is allowed to see, and a 'private' collection, about which one only hears rumors. And that private collection contains some works that, shall we say, were not necessarily obtained legally."

"You mean he has stolen paintings in his private collection? I've heard of that kind of thing. But I still don't see…"

"You will. It seems there's another such collector in Japan, whose name Rafael didn't learn, who's in possession of—I won't say 'owns,' because I doubt he got it legally—who has a Monet that Sanders would give anything to have, to add to his secret collection. Like Sanders, this man—let's call him Mr. Suzuki for the moment—doesn't need money—he just wants to add to his collection. Perhaps now you can guess what it is, in addition to paintings, that Mr. Suzuki collects."

"Uh, violins?" I hazarded.

"Right the first time. He collects rare musical instruments, and apparently one that he has coveted for a very long time is my Guarneri."

"Okay, I'm confused again. So this Japanese guy stole the violin?"

"No, Sanders did. You see, Sanders badly wants the Monet that Suzuki has; while Suzuki desperately wants the violin that—now—Sanders has."

"And they swapped, so the violin is in Japan now?" This did not sound promising for Aaron.

"I hope not. No, given the circumstances, it's not that easy to make such an exchange. Sanders doesn't want to send the violin to Japan until he has the painting, and Suzuki won't let the painting out of his sight until he has the violin in his hands and has examined it. Rafael understands that Suzuki will be paying Sanders a visit sometime next month. He thinks that's when the exchange will be made, although he doesn't know just how."

"So where is the violin now?" I asked. I was beginning to suspect just where Aaron was heading.

"Well, Sanders lives in California, but Rafael says Sanders doesn't have the violin yet. It's apparently still in the hands of the crook who actually stole it, guy named Donny Martin, who lives around here somewhere and who apparently is holding out for more money than he'd been promised."

After a long pause, during which Aaron looked down at his shoes and did not attempt to continue the story, I asked him, a bit warily, "Have we arrived yet at what you have in mind for me?"

Aaron looked up and smiled. "Well, yes, I suppose we have. I want to get that violin back before it goes to Japan."

"And you want to get it back by…by what means?"

"Well, until today, I didn't have a specific plan in

mind. But now that I've met you..."

I was afraid of that.

It was now my turn to be silent. I had to get this straight in my mind. Finally I asked, "Why not tell the police what you've learned and let them recover the violin? They could get a search warrant..."

Aaron waved that off. "First of all, by the time the police got the warrant and got around to using it, the violin would probably be in Sanders' hands. They would never invade Sanders' home, even if they had all the warrants in the world, certainly not without an absolutely concrete case against him. And in any event, I can't even tell them the name of my informant, because I promised him I'd keep it a secret. If Sanders found out...well, I'd never put him in that kind of position."

"I see. So you want me to...to recover your violin from Mr. Martin?" My eyes and my tone of voice both no doubt revealed a great deal of skepticism. It was not lost on Aaron.

"Well, yes, that was the idea I had. Recover the Guarneri and leave the copy in its place."

"Oh yes, the copy. Tell me about that."

"It's pretty simple. I wanted to complete my tour, and I was willing to take a chance that, playing in a big recital hall, most people in the audience would not be able to tell the difference between a very good violin and a Guarneri."

When my features assumed an even more skeptical pose, he continued: "After all, I played almost my whole life without the Guarneri, and no one ever complained. So long as I don't actually say I'm playing it, I'm not misrepresenting anything."

"Except your recitals have been written up in the newspaper with a detailed description of your instrument," I pointed out.

"Yes, well, I still didn't say I'd be playing it for every recital. In fact, on occasion I haven't been able to use it for one reason or another. Anyway, the fact remains that I didn't have any choice, other than to either cancel the recitals or announce I was playing a different violin. Then I'd have to explain about the theft, and that would become a big story and probably scare off the thief, and I might never see the violin again. So I decided to compromise."

"Compromise how?"

"Over the years, there have been several very good copies of Stradivarius and Guarneri violins made, some intended to fool a buyer and others just intended to look and sound as close as possible to the real thing. Similar to the excellent copies of famous paintings that show up from time to time for the same reasons. As you saw for yourself"—Aaron reached over and picked up the "fake" Guarneri—"at first glance the copy looks very authentic. It doesn't sound exactly the same, perhaps, but superficially it looks quite similar and it sounds very good. What's missing in this case, and I saw you were looking there, is the label. But of course that can only be seen close up."

"Yes," I said, "if I hadn't read up on how to identify the genuine article, I wouldn't have known."

"No. This violin wasn't intended to defraud anyone, it's just a very good copy, and the maker didn't bother with the label. Anyway, I know a dealer who has access to such copies, and I arranged with him to buy one. It cost me extra to get it immediately, but he managed."

I let all of this sink in. Finally, I said, "Okay, I think I understand. You want me to steal the real violin back from Sanders…"

"No, from Martin, if we can get to it in time, before it gets to Sanders. If not, then from Sanders."

"Right. Steal it back from Martin."

"And substitute this copy," Aaron added.

"Of course, Sanders'll know it's a copy as soon as he looks closely at it."

"I know that, but by that time it'll be too late."

"He won't be too happy with Mr. Martin, I should think."

"No. And if I'm really lucky, he won't examine it closely until he's ready to make the exchange with the Japanese fellow. That should prove mighty embarrassing for the son-of-a-bitch, don't you think?" Aaron broke out in a grin, the first time he had smiled since beginning his story of the theft.

I considered this. Then I said, "Yeah, I'd say so. And if the switch is done well, he won't have any idea how the original turned into a fake!"

Aaron brightened. "So you'll do it? You'll help me get my violin back?"

I held up a hand to stop the premature celebration. "Maybe. There's a lot of details we'd have to work out. Like whether the job is even doable, given the lay of the land and all; and what's in it for me." It occurred to me that I already owed Aaron for letting me off the hook, but this sort of thing would require an additional inducement.

"I don't know the layout, but I assume we could find it out. As for what's in it for you, I have no idea.

I've never hired a burglar before, and until you entered the picture an hour ago, I had no intention of doing so. What would be fair?"

I didn't have a ready answer for that.

"I don't ordinarily hire my services out, either. I usually work on my own. So we're both in virgin territory here. Let me think."

I sat back silently on my downy cushion, while Aaron got up and walked to the mini bar, where he poured us both refills. Then he sat back down and waited.

I couldn't come up with a good answer off the top of my head, so I said, "Maybe we should analyze the situation and see where it leads us."

"Okay by me. You go first."

I got up and began to pace. "Let's see. The violin is worth several million dollars, right?"

"Right."

"And I'd be putting myself in a very dangerous position, with regard to both Martin—and Sanders—and the law."

"Yes, I suppose so."

"You, on the other hand, would get all the benefit without any of the risk."

Here Aaron jumped up excitedly and waved me off.

"No, no, I think you misunderstand. I don't expect you to do this on your own.

"I want you to help me do it."

Chapter 6

I guess I looked surprised, because I was. I shook my head. "No thanks. I don't work well with others. Never have. My mother had to take me out of play groups because I couldn't share with my playmates. At school I got F's in 'Cooperates with Others'."

Aaron seemed unmoved. "No deal, then. This is a personal thing for me. I don't just want to get my violin back, but I'm sufficiently pissed off about having it stolen by that s.o.b. Sanders that I want to get it back myself. Now with professional help, of course," he said, nodding at me.

"But you'd be committing a crime. You could go to jail," I protested. I was beginning to think the guy was a nut case, although a likeable nut case.

Aaron shook his head. "Look, I'd be committing basically the same crime if I hired you to steal the violin as if I stole it myself, I know that much law. But it can't be much of a crime to take back what someone has just stolen from you. Maybe some minor trespass for entering his property. And besides, it's worth the risk. I won't let the bastard get away with it!"

Aaron had worked himself into quite a state, even pounding his fist into his palm to emphasize his last point. No doubt he generally saved this kind of emotion for the concert hall.

I let him vent, and when he was finished, I said,

"Sorry, but no way. You'd probably just get in the way. No offense, but you're an amateur. It would be like me trying to go out on stage and play a violin duet with you."

This seemed to bring Aaron up short. He considered my analogy, which was a pretty good one, if I do say so myself. I'm sure the very thought of appearing onstage in a duet with someone who had never played the violin before sent shivers down his spine.

"I see your point," he said quietly. "I can't blame you for not wanting to do this job with someone like me along."

I was relieved. I felt sorry for having to squelch Aaron's plan for personal revenge, but it couldn't be helped.

"I understand how you feel," I said, "but at least if I can get the violin back for you…"

"Oh, no," Aaron interjected before I could finish my sentence. "I can see why you wouldn't want to take me along, so I'll have to do it myself. No way I'm letting someone else do my dirty work for me!"

I was taken aback. "Are you serious?" He had to be joking.

"Absolutely. The more I think about it, the more determined I am to get that violin back, and to do it myself. It would have been great to have professional help, but since you're the only 'professional' I know, I'll just have to do without it."

I hardly knew what to say. Taking on this job with Aaron along would put us both at risk, and the logical thing to do was simply to thank him for his offer, and of course for not having me arrested for trying to steal his violin. But for reasons I could not quite explain to myself, the prospect of sending him off to do the job himself, with the near certainty that he would fail and end up in prison, or worse, appealed to me even less. I needed time to think.

"I'll tell you what," I said. "Give me overnight to think this through. It's kind of a new concept for me, you might say. Can we get together tomorrow?"

Aaron perked right up at the suggestion. "Sure. How about lunch here at the hotel?"

"Uh, if you don't mind, I'd rather not come back here for a while. I've led some people to believe I work here, and…"

"Oh sure, I understand. How about McCormick's?"

"Fine. I'll see you there at noon."

At least I would get a free lunch out of this.

Chapter 7

"Sara?"

"Oh, hi, Flo. What's up? How'd the great violin grab go?"

"Well, at the moment I'm sitting in my car in the parking lot of the Regency. I've just had the most bizarre experience of my short criminal career, and it's not quite over. I need some advice. Are you available?"

"You mean now? It would be a bit awkward." I heard a man's voice and then Sara giggled, and it wasn't from anything I had said. I got the message.

"Well, this evening would be okay. Can you come over about seven?"

"I think so. I'd planned on dropping in anyway. Can you give me a hint what this is about? I assume it has something to do with Aaron Levy."

"It has everything to do with Aaron Levy. And it's about whether I should let him stick his head in a noose, or I should accompany him into a noose for two.

"See you at seven."

****

Promptly at seven o'clock, Sara appeared at my door. She had a bottle of Merlot in one hand; the other was on her hip.

"Okay, it sounded like we're gonna need this," she said, thrusting the bottle into my hands. We retreated to the living room.

Sara and I settled ourselves on the sofa. Sara poured the wine.

"Okay," she said, "explain."

I did. I recounted briefly how I got into Aaron Levy's room, and in great detail my encounter with Aaron himself. It made quite a good story, punctuated by Sara with several repetitions of "No!," "Really?," and "You're kidding."

When I reached the part at which Aaron stated his determination to "go it alone," Sara switched to: "He's out of his mind!"

"That was my reaction, too," I said. "The only thing is, I believe he really intends to do it, or to try to do it, alone if he has to." I sighed. "In fact, he seems to be treating it like a challenge of some sort, like he's eager to prove he can do it."

"You know," Sara said, "I've read that famous violinists have a reputation for being gamblers. Something about their personalities. I believe Paganini once lost his priceless violin in a card game."

"This would be a much more dangerous game than cards," I said.

Sara agreed. "But what's that got to do with you? If he's crazy enough to break into a lion's den and try to steal the lion's prize violin...no, wait, I'm mixing my metaphors here...oh, you know what I mean. It's not your affair."

I looked down at my glass, then took a long sip.

"You're right, of course. It's just that he seems like such a nice guy, not at all what I'd expect a big celebrity to be like, and he did save me from my first stint at the license plate factory, and...well, I hate to leave him out there helpless. And believe me, he would be helpless! I'm sure he hasn't a clue how to steal a pencil from a blind beggar, much less a Guarneri from a wary billionaire."

"Millionaire," Sara said. "You said millionaire."

"Whatever. The point is, do I do the sensible thing and let him jump off the cliff by himself, or the stupid thing and jump off with him, hoping that two can fly better than one?"

Sara considered this.

"I don't know, Flo," she said after a long pause. "It's not like you never take chances in your, uh, line of work. In a way, this is just another risk, isn't it?"

"Sure it is, but the difference is that this is an unnecessary one. I can avoid it by refusing to take the job."

"You can, of course; but then the risk is that he'll get himself arrested, or even killed, and then you'll feel guilty as hell for the rest of your life." Usually so practical, Sara seemed to have taken Aaron's noble cause—or foolhardy adventure—to heart. At the very least, she was not trying to talk me out of jumping. In fact, it looked like no one was going to save me from what might easily turn out to be the most foolish venture I had ever undertaken.

Or the most exciting.

Or both.

****

Promptly at 12:30 p.m., a less-than-confident Florence Palmer entered McCormick's Fish House & Bar on Fourth Avenue. A throwback to the style and décor of the turn of the last century, McCormick's could induce nostalgia even in those too young to have actual memories of its wood and brass splendor. But I was too nervous to notice the elegance, as I looked around for Aaron. Spotting him at a corner table, I made my way there.

Aaron was reading the menu and looking quite serious about it when he looked up and saw me. His features brightened and he put down the menu, stood up, and went around to hold the chair for me. *That's unusual,* I thought. It's not a gesture I see very often these days.

After we'd been seated for a few minutes and had a chance to exchange a bit of small talk, a waitress came over to take a drinks order. Aaron ordered a bottle of champagne.

"What's the occasion?" I asked. I hoped he hadn't simply assumed I would agree to his proposition.

Apparently he hadn't. "Well," he answered, "at least one of us will have something to celebrate: You should be celebrating your escaping that close brush with the law, and perhaps I'll be celebrating your agreeing to help me to recover my violin. Either one calls for champagne."

I couldn't object to that. But whether Aaron had reason to celebrate was still an open question.

"Before we decide who's celebrating what," I said, "let's settle this matter of who's going to go after that violin."

Aaron was all smiles and attention and waited for me to continue. He sure seemed to be enjoying himself. I wished I could say the same.

"I've given it a lot of thought," I said, "and this is what I've decided: I have a list of conditions under which I might—and I say 'might'—be willing to do this job with you tagging along. If you're okay with all of them…"

As I seemed to run out of steam there, Aaron jumped in. "Then you'll do it?"

Reluctantly, I said, "Yeah, then I'll do it. Or at least take the next step, which would be trying to come up with a workable plan. Some things simply can't be done at all."

"I understand," Aaron replied eagerly. "So let's see this list."

"Before we go over the list," I said, holding up my hand to check his momentum, "we never did settle the matter of what's in this for me."

"That's right," agreed Aaron. "What did you decide would be fair?"

I cleared my throat. We were now talking business. "Well," I said, "given the value of the object, the degree of risk, and the financial circumstances of the client (you), I think $100,000 plus expenses would be fair." I had more or less pulled the figure out of the air, since I had no precedent for this job, and I waited to see what his reaction would be. I actually was expecting either a gasp of disbelief or an outright rejection, in which case I was ready to negotiate.

Aaron thought about my offer for a minute, with wrinkled brow. Then he said slowly, "And…what if we aren't successful? If we don't get the violin?"

"Then you just pay the out-of-pocket expenses, so I at least come out even." I started to add that he could also pay for our lawyer if we ended up in jail, but I refrained. I didn't want to sound too negative.

Again Aaron paused to think it over. Finally he brightened and said, "It's a deal! Now let's see the list."

****

I was relieved we had gotten past the first hurdle. I pulled out from my purse a folded page from my note pad. I looked at it and said, "First, once we have a plan, you have to stick to it, at least unless and until I say otherwise. No freelancing."

"I understand," Aaron said meekly. "Stick to the plan."

"Second, you have to learn a few techniques that every good burglar needs to know, and learn them damn fast. Like in a day."

"Hey, I'm a fast learner," Aaron assured me. "It said so on my report cards."

I was beginning to feel like an employer interviewing a young student for his first job. Come to think of it, when it came to crime, I was.

"And last but most important," I continued, "you have to promise to do exactly what I tell you during the operation itself, no matter whether you agree with it or not."

"Do exactly what the boss says," Aaron repeated. "No problem, SIR!" And here he snapped off a smart salute.

I was not amused. But I took that to be a "yes."

Suddenly Aaron's features became much more sober. "Seriously, Flo, I really want you to help me with this, and I'll do whatever you say. I don't have any trouble taking orders—spent two years in the Israeli army doing just that—and I know when I'm in over my head. That's why I want you there. Any other conditions?"

I glanced at my sheet of paper and shook my head. I looked up and said, "No, that's all I came up with, though I may think of something else along the way."

"So you'll do it?"

In my mind's eye, I could see the Rubicon rushing by in front of me. I hesitated for a moment, then stepped boldly onto the bridge and crossed the river. It was, in a way, a liberating thought. A new adventure was beginning, and with it the application of one more rule that I had not pressed upon Aaron: Make your decision, do the best you can, and never look back.

"Yeah," I said, smiling for the first time that day. "I'll do it.

"Now open the damn champagne!"

Chapter 8

Aaron had to leave Seattle for a short engagement down the coast, but he promised to be back in a day or two. After this gig, he said, he had nothing scheduled for at least two weeks and he had reserved his Royal Suite, no doubt at considerable expense, for the duration "as our base of operations." Not quite an army field office.

On the following Monday we began our quest in earnest.

Riding up in the hotel elevator with Aaron that morning—this time, of course, the guest rather than the service elevator—I couldn't quite shake the feeling that I was still an interloper. I was no longer in my frumpy housekeeper disguise, but I still wondered whether anyone would recognize me from my previous foray to the ninth floor. But in reality there wasn't much chance that anyone, even eager Assistant Manager Larry, would connect that menial servant with this well-dressed woman on the arm of the hotel's foremost celebrity guest.

Context—like timing—is everything.

Before we stepped out of the elevator on nine, I looked to see if any of the housekeepers who had been there on my previous visit were in the hallway now. But as it was well past the time for cleaning the suites, none of the maids were on the floor. Getting on the elevator as Aaron and I got off, however, was the bitch from room 914 who had complained to me about her unemptied wastebasket. Would she recognize the maid she had so recently abused at close range? I almost winced when we passed the woman, but I managed a curt nod, and in return I received a broad smile and a welcoming look that seemed to be evenly divided between good manners and envy. Context is indeed everything.

After Aaron poured drinks and we had settled into chairs on either side of the coffee table, I got out the sheet on which I'd written my conditions and turned it over to the blank side. Fishing out a pencil from my handbag, I looked up at Aaron and said, "Okay, now comes the hard part. How we're going to do this."

"You're the boss," Aaron said. "Where do we start?"

"I guess we start at Donny Martin's apartment," I said. "We'll have to find out where it is, then do a little reconnaissance."

"Right. So how do we find where Martin lives?"

I thought about that. How indeed.

"Well," I said, "I do know a few what you might call shady characters in town."

"Oh yes? How shady?"

"Let's just say we share some mutual business interests. Nice people, just engaged in questionable activities."

"Like yourself," Aaron said. But he was smiling when he said it.

"Like myself. To put it bluntly, if Martin is some kind of petty crook, he just might be known to other petty crooks."

"Then by all means get in touch with your crooked—sorry, I mean petty crooked—friends."

I took out my phone, checked the "contacts" list, and started calling. Surprisingly, it took only two phone calls to find Donny Martin's address. Or, as my friend Rolf put it, "That's assuming Donny ain't back in the slammer." There was always that possibility. I wonder whether they let you keep your priceless violin with you in your cell.

Rolf added that Martin lived with a roommate named Fred Ballard. He knew Ballard only casually, but from his tone he didn't think much of him.

"I think Ballard's been doin' time recently, attempted murder if I'm not mistaken, so he maybe ain't around. Or maybe he's out by now. Why'd you wanna know? I can assure you it ain't worth breakin' into that apartment—neither Martin or Ballard's got anythin' worth stealin'."

I laughed, both at Rolf's joke and the fact that if we were right, he was *so* wrong!

I thanked Rolf, promising to buy him a drink sometime.

Aaron said he would pick me up the next morning for step one in Operation Violin Recovery.

****

At eight a.m. the next morning we arrived at the apartment building where, according to my friend Rolf, Donny Martin and his roommate lived. I say "apartment building," but that probably dignifies the hovel a bit too much. Its tenants seemed to prefer bedsheets as curtains and its owner, perhaps too embarrassed to be seen there, apparently kept himself and any of his employees—such as painters and repairmen—far away.

But we weren't there to rent an apartment, and probably the rundown condition of the building meant there were unsophisticated locks (if any locks at all) and no security cameras or burglar alarms. I wouldn't have been surprised if there were no doors, but that at least proved to be incorrect.

Aaron got out of the rented car and came around to open my door, a gesture, like his pulling out that chair for me in the restaurant, that I had seldom experienced and found quite charming. I'm sure when my mother was my age, it was still standard procedure. But I digress.

Martin's apartment was 2B, presumably on the second floor, and that's where we headed. This was only reconnaissance, so we merely strolled in through the (unlocked) front door, took the stairs to the second floor (there was an elevator, but I doubted it could be trusted), and walked down the corridor until we found 2B.

As I'd suspected, the apartment door had a lock set only one step above the antique skeleton keys you see made into jewelry these days. Of course, there might be a secondary night latch on the inside, and that could be dealt with if necessary, but I thought it unlikely given the state of the visible hardware.

Back downstairs, we left the way we'd entered and walked around to the back of the building, which faced an alley. A dilapidated fence, with several boards missing or leaning precariously, enclosed a mixture of trash cans and un-canned trash. Through the fence we could see two back doors, neither of which appeared to offer much resistance to a determined, or even an apathetic, burglar. There was also a fire escape outside each apartment's back window, which might serve just as well to escape from the law, should that become necessary.

Satisfied with the layout, Aaron and I made our way back to his car and returned to the hotel to plan our little escapade. I was still very nervous about letting Aaron come along, but I'd agreed to it and couldn't back out now. I wondered whether later, in retrospect, I would regret that decision.

Chapter 9

"Getting in won't be a problem," I told Aaron when we had settled into the Royal Suite's comfortable chairs again. "The trick will be making our move when Martin isn't there and isn't likely to walk in on us, as I've heard happened to an intimate acquaintance of mine just recently. Funny, she was also looking for a Guarneri." I gave Aaron a meaningful look.

Aaron laughed. "I doubt this fellow Martin would have as poor manners as the person you're referring to," he said. "But just in case, let's pick a time when that's not likely to happen. So just how do we determine when that is?"

"That's a good question," I said. "There are at least two ways to handle that. Either we find out when he goes to work—if he goes to work—or otherwise leaves his apartment each day, or we find a way to lure him out for the length of time we'll need for the job. The first way may take a little longer, but it's more certain than the second."

"Okay, so how do we find out when he leaves?"

"The only sure way is to spend a day or two observing his movements. If it's a regular pattern, we can plan around it. If not . . ."

"If not what?"

"If not, I'll think of something else," I said.

At least I hoped I would.

****

Bright and early the next morning, Aaron and I found ourselves parked across the street from Donny Martin's apartment building, trying to look as inconspicuous as possible. There was a small park on that side of the street, and from time to time we got out of the car and strolled in the park, always keeping an eye on the front entrance of the building. Rolf, the friend who told me where Martin lived, had also described him in some detail, so I was pretty sure I'd know him when I saw him. How many men living in that building could be over six feet tall with red hair, a red beard, and a penchant for flashy clothes? Only one, I hoped.

At about nine a.m., a tall man with red hair and beard, wearing a very smart but very loud track suit, left the apartment building and set off down the street. That had to be our man. We had expected Martin would drive away in his car, and we were prepared to follow, but instead he just kept walking. So we got out and walked too, on the opposite side of the street.

Martin walked quickly and it was all we could do to keep up. About six blocks later, he entered the local branch of one of those fitness chains. Apparently he wasn't going to work; he was going to work out.

After about an hour and a half, during which Aaron and I strolled back and forth several times, shared an ice cream cone from a nearby creamery, and looked at our watches innumerable times, Donny Martin finally emerged from the gym, no doubt even more buff than when he arrived.

Once again we followed behind at a discreet distance until Martin disappeared inside his apartment building and, presumably, inside Apartment 2B.

From the lobby of Aaron's hotel, I telephoned Donny Martin's gym. A man answered with an enthusiasm reserved for the young and extremely healthy.

"Hi," I began in the sexiest voice I could summon. "I understand my friend Donny Martin is a regular at your gym."

"Yeah," Young and Healthy answered. "He's here most every day. Why d'ya wanna know?"

"I have something I want to give him and I'm wondering whether you can tell me if he's likely to be there tomorrow morning, so I can deliver it. I just missed him today."

There was a slight pause, perhaps as Young and Healthy briefly considered whether he was authorized to give out this sensitive information. If so, he apparently decided he was, because he said, "Yeah, he usually comes in a little after nine, so if you're here about then, you should catch him."

"Thanks so much," I breathed in my best Marilyn Monroe voice. "I really appreciate your assistance. I'll be there in the morning."

And that was that.

****

Having established that Mr. Martin would likely be at the gym after nine a.m. the next morning, that's when we decided to make our move.

"Getting into Martin's apartment should be a simple operation," I told Aaron, "as should finding the violin. So I'll take on that part of the job."

"Wait a minute," Aaron protested. "I thought we had a deal that we'd do this together. I won't…"

"Don't get your shorts in a twist. You'll have a very important job, in some ways more important than mine."

"Which is?" He didn't sound convinced.

"Which is lookout, to be sure Martin doesn't come home before I'm finished and out of the apartment. Just about the worst nightmare for any burglar is being caught in the act by the rightful owner of the merchandise she's about to make off with. And having that happen twice in succession might be more than my system can take."

"Fair enough. So you want me to stand outside the building and let you know if Martin comes back early?"

"Not exactly. I want you to drop me off, then go back and park across from the gym, so you can give me a warning when and if he leaves early. If you phone me and say he's on his way, I'll make sure I'm outta there within three or four minutes, regardless whether I've got the violin or not. Better to run away and live to burgle another day."

"And do I sit there and wait for you?"

"Hell no. You get your ass back here as fast as the speed limit allows, passing Martin on the way I assume, and pick me up at the back of the building. In other words, you keep me, and maybe you, out of the pokey. Is that important enough?"

Aaron looked appropriately contrite. "Yeah, I guess so. If someone has to be the lookout and someone the burglar, I suppose I'm the logical lookout. I was hoping to be in on the actual heist, but…"

"But you've been watching too much TV. Crime is like any other business. It takes good planning, trained personnel, and everyone doing their assigned job. To go back to my example of our playing a violin duet, that would work fine so long as you were doing the playing and I was turning the pages.

"Now let's go get some sleep. We have an early performance to play."

****

Since we had a tight schedule to keep, Aaron and I both slept in his suite, him in the king-size bed in the bedroom and me on the pull-out sofa in the front room. Yes, I know what you're thinking, but this was strictly business, whatever either of us might otherwise have had in mind.

The alarm clock went off the next morning at six a.m. I won't say I was bright-eyed and bushy-tailed, but I did manage to pry my eyes open and get my tail into my black-on-black work outfit.

Aaron was a different story. This man was clearly used to working late in the day—few concerts begin at nine in the morning—and therefore getting out of bed well after six. So I had to resort to the tried and true method of persuasion: I poured a glass of cold water over his head.

It did the trick.

I won't repeat here the manner in which Aaron thanked me for my assistance in getting him up and ready for action, but you can be certain it was both colorful and heartfelt.

"You're welcome," I said when he had come up for air. "You've hired a full service burglar."

I'm not sure Aaron was terribly appreciative of the service, but I just ignored him and checked that I had all necessary paraphernalia: lock picks, screwdriver, flashlight, cell phone. When Aaron was finally alert and dressed, I made sure he had his necessary kit: car keys and cell phone.

We were ready to roll.

****

One thing you can't predict with accuracy is traffic, especially in Seattle. I had made sure we started out with plenty of extra time—half an hour—to arrive before nine at Martin's apartment. As it happened, it wasn't enough.

My mistake was getting on the freeway instead of relying on the slower city streets. Just our luck, there was an accident ahead of us, and we were stuck with nowhere to go, no way to get off the freeway, until it cleared enough for a single lane of traffic to get by. So we arrived at the apartment building about 9:10. We waited in front for several minutes, but no Martin came out the door. A couple of men left the building and one woman, but no one meeting Martin's description.

"Shall we just wait and hope he's running late, like us?" Aaron asked as the minutes ticked by.

"I don't think so," I said. "It's twenty after already. I assume we missed him. He was on time and we weren't. Drop me off and head for the gym for your lookout duties. I'll go and get the violin."

Aaron dropped me off at the back of the building. I found the rear entrance door, which was conveniently unlocked. Who would want to break into this dump?

Upstairs to apartment 2B. Since we weren't absolutely certain Martin had left for the gym—maybe he overslept and was just getting into his workout togs—I rapped on the door loudly enough for someone inside to hear, hoping not to arouse the neighbors. Had he answered the door, I was prepared with Plan B, a

"Sorry, wrong floor" excuse, although I would have regretted his having seen me, should I later show up in a police lineup. This was unlikely, as thieves don't generally go to the police to report that their stolen property had been stolen from them. Anyway, there was no response, so I proceeded with Plan A.

I had no trouble at all picking the old, outdated lock in the doorknob. There was no dead bolt.

There was, however, a dead body.

Chapter 10

I won't say I've never seen a dead person before, but then it had only been at funerals. In those circumstances, not only is seeing the deceased to be expected, but pains have been taken to present him (or her) looking their very best—well scrubbed, dignified dress, the works. That is not what Donny Martin looked like, sprawled face down on the floor of his apartment, blood covering most of his back and a good part of what once passed for carpet. The last time I'd seen him, his most noticeable features were his red hair and beard. Red was still the dominant color, but this time it created a hideous clash between the electric blue shirt he was wearing and the ugly patch of blood on his back. The flashy dresser in him would never have approved.

The first thing I did was sit down heavily on the nearest chair. This was no time to be either sick or panicky, no matter how I was feeling.

The violin. That was what I'd come for. Was it here?

I looked up and surveyed the apartment, avoiding looking in the direction of the deceased. The room I was in seemed to be a combination living room and kitchen. The former was a misnomer, as the tenant wasn't living. And while there was a small sink and appliances in one corner, the entire area was so piled with what appeared to be pizza boxes and empty beer bottles, I doubt anything had been cooked there since Martin moved in.

There were no pictures on the walls, and what passed for carpets were threadbare. The overriding atmosphere, wholly apart from the corpse in front of me, was gloom, and I wanted out of there ASAP. I could see that the only window in the room was wide open, probably because whoever shot Martin had exited that way. I was sorely tempted to do the same. Nevertheless, I dutifully arose and walked around, giving Donny a wide berth, checking every shelf and opening every door, looking for the violin. One door led to a bedroom, with an unmade bed and the acrid aroma of unwashed linens. I held my breath and checked under the bed and in the closet. No violin.

Hadn't I gone through this once before, quite recently, in a very different kind of apartment?

Back in the living room, I made one more look around, but still no violin.

So was it the violin that was behind the murder? Had Donny Martin gambled he could squeeze more money out of Sanders for the violin he stole from Aaron? If so, someone was playing for much higher stakes.

****

Obviously, there was no longer a need for a lookout, and I immediately took out my cell phone and called Aaron. Before he could get beyond "Hello," I blurted out, "Get here as fast as you can. Pick me up in back. Don't ask questions." That last was because he was about to say something, and conversation I didn't need right then.

Just as I hit "end call" on my phone, someone

began knocking on the apartment door—knocking very loudly, followed by the words "police" and "open up." Caught by surprise and in a situation I'd never been in before, I did what any red-blooded American lady burglar would do: I panicked.

I rushed for the open window—there had to be a fire escape under it, right?—but in my haste I dropped my phone near Martin's body. I reversed course and retrieved it. When I bent down, I saw lying next to the phone what appeared to be a man's ring. For some reason I picked it up. It was quite heavy and had the initials "BJD" on it. Obviously not Donny Martin's. I wiped the blood off it, getting some on my hands, and put it in my pocket.

By that time, two men in blue had burst through the unlocked door and there I was, literally caught red-handed.

I surrendered without a fight.

****

I'm usually pretty good at coming up with innocent explanations for guilty circumstances, right from when my mother would catch me with my hand in the cookie jar. ("Just putting back the cookie I found on the counter, Mom.") But I admit this one had me at a total loss. All I could think to say was, "I didn't do it."

Apparently that wasn't a sufficient explanation for the officer who seemed to be in charge. While his partner checked to confirm Martin was indeed deceased and phoned in a request for medical backup, he wanted a few more details. Such as:

Him: "What the hell's going on here?"

Me: "This man seems to have been shot, officer."

Him: "I can see that. Who are you?"

Me: "Well, I'm a…a friend. No, not exactly a friend, more like a stranger."

Him: "What're you doing here?"

Me: "I wish I knew. I guess the door was open and I just walked in and . . ."

Needless to say, I was not making a very good impression. After several minutes, as the officers waited for their backup and I waited to be executed, Aaron appeared outside the open door. He'd come back for me and, not finding me waiting in the alley, he'd come upstairs to look for me. Fortunately, when he saw through the open door the body in dappled red, the police in blue, and the idiot in black, he quickly figured out that was no place for him, and he kept on walking down the corridor.

I was glad to see him go.

I figured he'd be back.

****

Having regained just a bit of my wits, there was something I just had to know. So I asked the officer in charge how they happened to be on the scene so quickly.

"I mean, I'm really glad you showed up—I was just about to call you—but it turned out I didn't have to. How come?"

"Just lucky, I guess," he said with a rueful smile. "Lady in the next apartment apparently heard raised voices coming from this place and then what sounded like a gunshot, which unfortunately ain't that uncommon in this neighborhood. Worried about it for a while and finally phoned 911. We were the closest car to the scene, so we showed up. Like I said, just lucky."

Some luck. But that explained it.

Timing is everything.

I won't bore you with the sordid details of my trip "downtown" and the first booking of my career. Let's just say it was both scary and humiliating and leave it at that.

Fortunately, I was not charged with murder, at least not yet. The police knew they had a weak case, as there was no murder weapon to be found—and believe me, they made a thorough search inside and outside the apartment. But I was the best suspect they had, and besides, given my black ninja outfit and the lock picks and other paraphernalia they found on me, they figured I was up to something illegal. They booked me on suspicion of burglary, although I think they really suspected I had somehow murdered Martin and disposed of the gun. Swallowed it, I suppose.

I was going to use my "one phone call" (assuming a person really gets one and that's not just something they say in the movies) to call Aaron, but I didn't have to bother. Almost as soon as I arrived at the police station, Aaron, who obviously had been watching developments and following the police car I was in, walked in and inquired how I might be released. Given the relatively minor nature of the charge, despite what they might actually suspect, and my clean record, despite all the burglaries they were thankfully unaware of, bail was set according to a standard schedule rather than my having to wait to see a judge the next day.

I didn't know how much it cost Aaron to bail me out, but of course whatever it was, he could well afford it; and besides, he owed it to me. After all, I was really just his employee, and surely posting bail is a standard employee benefit.

When all the necessary papers had been signed and funds transferred, Aaron and I walked out into the sunshine that I'd been afraid I wouldn't be seeing for quite a while.

On the way to Aaron's car, I gave him a hug and a little kiss on the cheek and thanked him for extricating me from the pokey and doing it so quickly. He looked a bit embarrassed by that, but he cleared his throat and said in his best businesslike manner:

"Okay, so why'd you shoot him, and where'd you put the violin?"

Chapter 11

I was tempted to make up some kind of sordid story about how I had shot Martin, swallowed the gun, and tossed the violin out the window, but I decided just to tell him the truth, which was almost as bizarre. So I just laughed—mirthlessly, as they say—and waited until we were driving away from the city jail before I responded.

"Obviously, I didn't kill Martin," I said as I tried to get comfortable. It was warm out and my black jumpsuit was not the ideal fashion for the occasion. "He was quite dead when I got there. And there was no violin—I looked everywhere before the police arrived."

"And that's another thing," Aaron interrupted. "How did they know there'd been a murder there?"

I explained what the officer had told me.

"How long do you think it took the police to get there?" Aaron asked.

"I'm not sure, but I got the impression that Martin hadn't been dead for long. And the police probably assumed it was a nosy neighbor with a vivid imagination and so weren't in a particular hurry to get there."

"Yeah, I suppose so. Anyway, if Martin's been shot and the violin's missing, it seems pretty clear who killed him, and why."

"You mean Sanders? You think a man in his

position would murder someone just to get a valuable violin?"

"Well, no, I guess not. But since the violin is gone, he must've been killed for that. And who else knew he had it?"

"Except us, you mean," I pointed out.

"Yes, except us. And I don't mean Sanders came up here and did the job himself, any more than he stole the violin himself. Just that he had it done for him."

"Okay, but isn't it possible someone else found out about it—saw it in his apartment, maybe—and killed him for it?" I said.

"I guess so, "Aaron said, "but what're the odds that someone spotted the violin and recognized it as a priceless Guarneri?"

I then told Aaron about the ring I found near Martin's body.

"Let's see it," he said. "It might be a clue to who killed Martin."

"I gave it to the police," I said. "Or rather they found it when they searched my pockets."

"Hmm. Well, I guess if it helps them find the killer . . . ."

"Or maybe helps us find him. The guy it belongs to has a pretty hefty hand and the initials 'BJD.' Maybe we can match it up. Of course we can't be sure the owner of the ring killed Martin," I pointed out, "just that he was in the apartment."

"Unless Martin stole the ring," Aaron said, "and it has nothing to do with his being killed."

"That's true. But then why would it be next to his body, with blood on it?"

"I don't know," Aaron said, "but rings don't easily

fall off fingers."

I thought about this for a moment. "Unless it wasn't on the killer's finger…"

"What do you mean?"

"Oh, nothing. Anyway, that ring is one of the few clues we have, even if it isn't very helpful."

"So are we back at square one?" He scratched his head.

I gave it one more try. "Maybe it was Martin's roommate who killed him—if he's not in jail—or maybe Martin blabbed about it to friends, maybe while he was drunk…"

"Okay, okay, there are a million possibilities. We don't know for sure who killed Martin, or whether Sanders now has the violin. But if he has it, it's likely he had Martin killed for it. Of course, we'll have to wait a few days, so whoever took it from Martin has time to deliver it to Sanders. I'll contact Rafael again and hope he can find out."

It suddenly occurred to me where this conversation was headed.

"Wait just a minute," I said. "Assuming we find that Sanders now has the violin, you aren't still intending to steal it back from him, are you? I mean, now that we know he plays for keeps and doesn't mind killing people to hang onto that fiddle?"

"Absolutely," Aaron said, sounding like he meant it. "Nothing has really changed, except the job is maybe a little more risky than it was."

"'A little more risky'? A little? You call getting shot a little more risky than merely being caught stealing a violin?"

"Okay, more than a little. And I won't hold you to

our bargain if you want out. But stealing it is still the only way to get it back."

I thought about this, but not for long.

"How about we tell the police the real reason we were in Martin's apartment—"

"Excuse me, why *you* were in Martin's apartment. You wouldn't let me go with you."

"Okay, why I was in Martin's apartment, about the violin being stolen by Sanders, and help them find the killer, and at the same time your violin."

Aaron shook his head. "You forget that we still have absolutely no evidence to link Sanders with the theft, much less with the killing. All we'll get is maybe a lawsuit for defamation. At the very least, we'd be telling the police that you were in Martin's apartment to steal a violin, and that I hired you to do it. Not exactly the kind of thing we'd like them to know. No, it's still up to us—sorry, to me—to get that violin back."

So here we were right back where we were in Aaron's suite, except this time while the rewards had stayed the same, the risks had gone up considerably. Or so I thought until Aaron reminded me that the reward side had changed as well:

"And there's another, maybe more important reason not to quit now. You've been arrested at the scene of the crime, standing over the body, with no good excuse for being there. At least none the police are aware of. And while you weren't charged with murder yet, you can be sure you're still suspect number one, because you're their only suspect. If it weren't for the fact they can't find the gun, I think you'd have been charged with murder by now."

You can bet that sent a shiver down my spine.

Aaron sure knew how to cheer a woman up.

"It seems to me," Aaron continued, "the only way to clear your name for certain is to find out who really shot Martin. If it was some unknown person, like, as you just suggested, someone who found out about his having it, there's not much we can do to find him. But if whoever killed Martin took the violin to bring it to Sanders, we can best find him at the source, so to speak. I think we'll find that person where we find Sanders."

Obviously there were several holes in Aaron's theory, but I was in no mood or condition to argue with him. He did have a point. Unless the cops could find the real killer of Donny Martin, I was still their best alternative. And although I was probably being somewhat uncharitable toward them, I couldn't help thinking that the police might rather convict a possibly innocent suspect than appear to let a serious crime go unsolved.

So it would be up to me to decide whether to carry on after this disastrous start, or to jump this sinking ship.

Loyal crew member or deserting rat.

****

Aaron took me back to his suite, where we sat across from each other, each sipping a scotch and soda. I'm sure I needed it more than he did, but of course it was a rough day for both of us.

"Let's wait until I can talk with Rafael," Aaron said after the silence became a bit thick. "If he can't find out whether Sanders now has the violin, there's no point in proceeding further."

"What will you do then?" I asked.

"What can I do? I'll have to tell the police about

the theft and hope they can somehow find the violin, if not the thief."

"And the murder? What happens to me?"

"Yes, that's a bit tricky, isn't it?" he said. "If I tell them I thought Martin's murder was because he had the stolen violin, they'll want to know how I know that, which would lead to either telling them who told me Martin had it, or telling them that we tried to steal it back, or both."

"Which would give us both a motive to kill Martin," I pointed out. "Anyway, I can't think about this any more today. I need a hot shower and an early bedtime."

Chapter 12

I had that hot shower as soon as I got home, but I didn't go right to bed. I had to tell someone about what had happened that day, and of course Sara was the one I had to tell.

"So Aaron had to bail you out," Sara said after I had poured us some Chardonnay and gone over the events from knocking on Martin's door to driving home with Aaron. "And a dead body! You poor thing—what a terrible experience. You're lucky you weren't the one getting shot. I assume you've had enough of this caper and are ready to resume your nice, quiet burglary business. Or maybe even go straight?"

"Not so fast," I said. "It's more complicated than that. Aaron still intends to go after his violin himself, whether I go with him or not. And as he pointed out, I'm now a prime suspect in Martin's killing, so in addition to recovering Aaron's violin, I have to try to discover who really killed Martin, the answer to which Aaron thinks lies with Sanders or his henchmen. So things haven't really changed that much."

"Yeah, except now it seems you might end up dead, instead of just in jail."

She was right, and I didn't argue the point.

"Okay, so this is different. I'll have to cross that bridge when I come to it. And maybe Aaron's friend will report that the violin still hasn't shown up at

Sanders' house, in which case I won't have to cross the bridge at all."

This thought kept me from obsessing on the possibility of putting my head back in the noose I'd barely escaped.

Until, that is, the next morning at 10 a.m. when Aaron telephoned. At least he let me sleep in after my exhausting, not to mention humiliating, experience as a perp.

"How're you feeling?" he asked, sounding genuinely concerned.

"About like you'd expect," I said, "after finding a dead body I wasn't expecting, not finding a stolen violin I was expecting, and finding myself suspected of burglary and maybe murder. Lousy."

Silence. Then, "That bad, huh?"

"That bad."

"So where do we go from here?"

"Not to the Bay Area, if that's what you're thinking," I said.

"But I'm sure that's where the violin must be now," Aaron said, sounding almost as if he actually believed it.

"Yeah, like you were sure it was in Donny Martin's apartment."

"And I'm still sure it was," Aaron insisted, "and that whoever murdered Martin took the violin. Or to put it more precisely, Martin was murdered because he had the violin. I'm sure of it. Otherwise it would still have been there."

"Well, then I hope you're sure of who killed him, because right now the police think I did. And before we worry about who has the violin, let's worry about who killed Martin, so your friendly neighborhood burglar doesn't end up at the end of a rope."

"They don't hang people anymore," Aaron said.

I hated it when Aaron became pedantic.

"Look," I said, "I don't give a shit whether they'd hang me, electrocute me, or throw me to the lions. I'd be equally dead. What I do give a shit about is finding who did kill Martin."

"Well," Aaron said, sounding at least slightly chastened, "I assume the police are trying to find out just that."

"Maybe so," I said, "but their incentive isn't half as great as mine, and like I said, I think they already believe it was me. They just don't have enough evidence yet."

Again silence, and then, "Fair enough. So do you think it was Sanders, or someone working for Sanders, who killed Martin? If Martin was trying to squeeze Sanders for more money…"

"I don't know what I think right now. Listen, can we get together somewhere and talk this over? And decide what to do next?"

"I guess…"

"And yes, I know how important getting that violin back is to you. But first things first, and as far as I'm concerned, keeping me above ground and unincarcerated—is there such a word?—keeping me outta jail is the first thing."

"Okay," Aaron said. "Your place or mine?"

"Yours has much softer furniture. How about noon, and we'll order room service for lunch?"

"Works for me. Phone when you're in the lobby so I can come get you."

I'd forgotten about the heavily guarded Concierge floor. I'd need an escort.

"Bring your magic key," I said. "See you then."

****

Back in those comfy chairs in Aaron's suite.

"So how are we supposed to find out who killed Martin?" Aaron asked. "We know almost nothing about him, never met him…" For a person who had seemed up until now nothing but positive, Aaron was sounding awfully negative about the Donny Martin branch of the violin caper.

"I think we have to try," I said. "Maybe we can at least turn up enough information to point the police in the right direction. Or any direction other than toward me. Remember, they're operating without the somewhat relevant information about your stolen violin. In other words, we know the motive, at least what we think was the motive. Now if you want to tell them about the violin…"

"We've been over that," Aaron said, a bit testily, I thought. "That would give both of us a motive and get my friend in trouble and…"

"Yes, yes. So let's go over what we do and don't know, and see if it gets us anywhere."

"Well," said Aaron, scratching the back of his head and squinting, "we believe Martin is the thief who initially stole the violin from my car." He ticked this point off on his index finger. I took notes on a pad I'd brought along. "And we believe he stole it on the orders of, or at least at the behest of, Sanders." Point number two on his middle finger. "And if the information from Rafael is correct, Martin was holding out for a bigger payoff." Point three, ring finger. "So maybe he got a bigger payoff than he expected."

"Maybe. So that obviously points to Martin being killed by Sanders, or someone hired by Sanders," I said. "And if that's so, Sanders must have used either someone inside his organization or someone outside, sort of a hired gun."

"Like Martin," Aaron said. "And he saw how well that worked out."

"Okay, never mind that, it's still Sanders behind it, whoever he used. If we could prove that, it'd be sufficient to get me off the hook. Now who else might it have been if it wasn't Sanders or someone he put up to it?"

Aaron looked thoughtful again. At last he said, "Well, it *could* have been just an ordinary case of burglary and homicide, or someone Martin had pissed off or cheated—"

"Or double-crossed."

"Yes, or double-crossed, since he seemed inclined that way."

"But if that's the case," I said, "I doubt we'd have any chance of finding out who it was. Besides, the violin was gone, and it's hardly the kind of thing someone would bother to steal unless they knew how valuable it was. So let's cross that possibility off for now and stick to what we do know. How about that roommate of his, what was his name?"

"Hmm. Ballard, I think. Hank Ballard?"

"No, you're thinking of the singer. Fred Ballard, that was it. Maybe he did it."

"But I thought your contact said Ballard was in jail."

"Yeah, for attempted murder, I think. But what if

he's out? Rolf only said he thought Ballard might still be in jail. He didn't know. Maybe he came back to the apartment and Martin told him about the violin job, showed him the violin, and Ballard decides to take it and make a deal for himself. Martin tries to stop him, and…"

"Okay, I see your point," Aaron said, waving his arm to indicate he'd heard enough. "Let's pursue that line for a minute. It sounds pretty plausible. So Ballard shows up, Martin tells him about the violin deal, Ballard wants a cut, Martin refuses so Ballard decides to take the whole prize for himself, shoots Martin. Now he can't stay in the apartment, so he goes…where?"

Of course, that was the sixty-four dollar question, and I considered it. "Hmm. Well, if it were me—and I don't claim to know how the criminal mind works, despite the fact I could be considered a criminal myself—I'd get out of Dodge, far out, and close to where the money is."

Aaron nodded as he stood up and paced the floor. "You mean close to where Sanders lives, in California."

"Yes. It hardly pinpoints his location," I said, "but at least it gives us a starting point. And it means whichever theory we choose to chase down—Sanders had Martin killed or the roommate killed Martin so he could make the deal with Sanders—it takes us down to California, where we just might find both the killer and the violin."

I knew this was the conclusion Aaron wanted to reach, so he didn't have to put off going after his violin in order to pursue Martin's killer. And I had to agree it made sense.

"Okay," I said, "so we still need to know if the

violin is in fact with Sanders. Maybe your friend Rafael, or my friend Rolf, will have heard something. Maybe Ballard's already contacted Sanders to make a deal. So what do we do next?"

Aaron sat down again and tapped his right hand on the arm of the chair. He certainly seemed to be the twitchy sort when thinking. I was mentally attributing it to his violin playing when I found myself doing the same thing. So much for that theory.

"I think we should plan to make a trip to the Bay Area as soon as we find out Sanders has the violin," Aaron said. "If we find the violin, we might be able to find out how it got there, maybe who brought it to Sanders. Who knows? It might be someone we haven't even considered. But if they have—or had—the violin, they probably killed Martin."

I nodded agreement. "Ideally what we want, of course, is the murder weapon, to match up with the bullet that killed Martin. I don't know how we'd get it, but if we can learn where—or whose—it is, we might come up with a way."

"That'd be great, but a long shot. Anyway, I'll check with Rafael and ask him to let us know as soon as the violin shows up."

"If it shows up," I said. And then suddenly I thought of a small problem.

"Wait a minute," I said. "If I recall correctly, one of the terms of my bail bond is that I can't leave the state. Last I looked, Seattle was in Washington and the Bay Area was in California."

Aaron considered this.

"That's right," he said. "But of course there's no way they're going to know you've traveled to

California, unless they check all the airline passenger lists every day looking for you, which I doubt. As long as you show up for your hearing when it's scheduled, which I believe isn't for another month or so, you should be fine. And besides, what's the worst that can happen? I lose a whole lot of money and you get put back in jail."

"You make it sound so innocuous," I said. "How about if I lose the money and you get put in jail?"

"You got fifty thousand dollars cash handy?"

I gasped. "You mean it cost you fifty thousand dollars to spring me from the pokey?"

"Sure did."

I gave Aaron a big kiss on the cheek. "Thank you," I said.

"So are you willing to chance their finding out you've left the state?"

I could hardly say no, as I definitely wanted to find out who killed Martin, not to mention earn that hundred grand for recovering Aaron's violin.

So I said yes.

Chapter 13

It was about two days later that Aaron phoned again. He sounded excited.

"Guess what?" he said. "Guess who I just talked to."

"Your mother? Your accompanist?"

"No, no. I just talked with Rafael, down in Los Altos, where Sanders lives. He says Sanders should have the violin in a couple of days. And he knows who's got it, and who's going to bring it to Sanders."

"Really? Who?"

"Rafael."

"Yeah, I know you're talking about Rafael, but who's bringing the violin?"

"I just told you. Rafael. Come on over and I'll explain. And get ready to pack your bags."

****

A half hour later I was again in Aaron's suite, sunk into a chair I was beginning to consider my personal piece of furniture. I had a gin and tonic in my hand, and Aaron, sitting across from me, was holding straight bourbon.

"So tell me already," I said, "what the hell you're talking about. What did Rafael say?"

"Well, it's like this. Apparently we were right about who killed Martin and took the violin, because this guy Ballard, Martin's former roommate, contacted

Sanders, or at least the Sanders residence, saying he had the violin and was willing to part with it for whatever Sanders had offered Martin."

"Wait a minute. Does this mean Sanders hired Ballard to get the violin from Martin, or that Ballard acted on his own?"

"I don't know," Aaron said. "And I doubt it matters to Sanders, as long as he gets his—that is, my—violin, on his terms."

"Okay. So the violin is in Sanders' hands?"

"Not exactly. Sanders is away somewhere on business for a few days, and apparently he wants to be there in person when the violin arrives. So he doesn't want it delivered until he gets back."

"And then he'll have Ballard deliver it to him?"

"Also not exactly. But this is the good part. Ballard insisted someone come to where he's staying, bringing the cash. He didn't want to be in the enemy camp, where they could grab the violin and send him off empty-handed, or worse. Much worse. So Sanders is having Rafael retrieve the violin from Ballard. Apparently Rafael is pretty reliable, and not likely to take off with the cash instead of giving it to Ballard. So Sanders filled Rafael in on the violin plan, much of which of course he already knew, and told him he'd be the go-between."

"Sounds good," I said. "But wait: If Rafael is picking up the violin, why not just have him bring the violin to you instead of Sanders? That'd save everyone—meaning you and me—a helluva lot of trouble."

"I thought of that, of course, but I quickly realized I'd be putting Rafael in an untenable position.

Remember, I promised I wouldn't even disclose that he told me about the violin, because of what Sanders—or someone on his behalf—might do if he found out. Think what he might do if he found out Rafael had double-crossed him. Remember there's already been one murder over my violin."

"Okay, I get that. So we just have to wait until the violin is actually in Sanders' possession to begin our little retrieval mission."

"Right. We should plan to head for the Bay Area pretty soon. But I want to wait until I'm sure the violin is there, in Sanders' possession.

"And besides," he added, "I have some…some business to attend to in the next day or two. Meanwhile you can be coming up with a plan for our little escapade, since you're the professional here."

At least he recognized who was in charge. Or maybe he just didn't want to be bothered with the planning end of things. One way or the other, it was three days later before Aaron called again.

"It's official," he said. "Sanders definitely has the violin. I just spoke with Rafael, and like I told you, he's the one who retrieved it from Ballard."

That all sounded fine, although somehow Aaron didn't sound especially pleased that we would now be heading for the Bay Area to retrieve his prized possession.

Either he's getting cold feet, which would be more than understandable for even an experienced burglar, or he's finally realizing this is not fun and games, but a serious job that requires careful planning and a sober attitude.

"Good news," I said, though I wasn't entirely sure

myself that it was. This could be a fool's mission, even if a necessary one. "Let's get together tomorrow and make final plans."

"Roger and out," he said, and hung up.

Strange man. But in a nice way.

Chapter 14

Morning, in Aaron's suite. I was becoming as regular a visitor as the maid I almost was.

Aaron sounded more upbeat than he had on the phone, which was good to hear.

An earlier-than-usual glass of wine in hand to bolster my own nerves, I laid out the plan I had formulated.

"First, I need all of the information that you have available, even trivial-seeming details, about this Sanders guy and where he lives. I can't tell now what little detail will turn out to be crucial in some unexpected way."

"Fair enough." Aaron got up and went over to the closet, where he extracted a thin leather briefcase. He brought it back to the coffee table, opened it, and took out some notes, then laid it aside. Glancing at the notes, he said, "Sanders is very wealthy. He's apparently one of these millionaires who grew up poor, made a ton of money in his 40's, and now he's fifty-something and spending it like it's going out of style."

"On things like stolen violins?"

"And paintings and whatever else catches his fancy. But not all stolen by any means. Most of his collection is quite legit."

"Is he married?"

"No, at least not now. In fact, from what I can

gather, he's one of those lecherous moneybags who picks up sweet young things here and there, plays with 'em for a while, then pays them off and moves on to the next one. Or two or three."

"You mean plays with them in bed."

"Well, I don't mean chess or Monopoly. Yes."

"Okay," I said, "I've got a picture of the guy, although I'll need an actual photo as well."

"You can get one off the internet."

"Fine. Let's move on for the moment to his house, where I assume we'll find your violin?"

"Right. Later today I'll ask Rafael for as detailed a plan of the house, and where in it we might find the violin, as he can give me. He should be able to get it to me overnight. What I do know is that Sanders' house is not far from San Francisco. It's in Los Altos, one of those expensive suburbs."

"The sooner the better," I said. "We'll have to do a certain amount of reconnaissance, not only of the house, but of the area around it, since we won't be familiar with the territory. I'd estimate the whole operation will require a minimum of, say, two weeks."

Aaron didn't look happy about my estimate. "Hmm…we may have a problem here. I don't want to lose any time, because the longer we wait, the more likely the violin might be transferred to the Japanese collector. But I've got a recital series in L.A. this coming week, and that'll take up at least three or four days; then I'm free for several weeks. Maybe you could get started on your own?"

I thought about that for a few moments, then shook my head.

"I don't know. I really think setting up this job

requires more than one person. I'm also a little concerned that even if we're both there, we won't have any 'back-up'."

"What kind of back-up?"

"Well, if something goes wrong, as it well might, we'd have no one to contact to help us out."

"Are you suggesting we add a third person to the job? I don't get it. First you say you only work alone, then you reluctantly let me come along, and now you want to add someone—"

"No, not exactly. Let me explain. I do work alone. But I have this good friend named Sara I've known for years, who knows what it is I do and who has occasionally helped me out of jams I've gotten myself into. I'd sure like her to come along to the Bay Area with us."

"But is it a good idea to let someone else in on our plans, even a friend of yours?"

"Hey, it's too late for that. Sara already knows all about you and the violin. In fact, she helped me decide to let you come along on the job."

Aaron smiled. "Well, in that case, by all means invite the lovely lady along."

"Unfortunately, it's not quite that easy. Even though Sara sometimes shares with me what you might call the joys of victory and the agony of defeat, she's always steadfastly refused to get directly involved in my 'business.' But she might be willing to help with the reconnaissance part, and I'd sure like the company."

"Tell her I'll pay her expenses as well as yours—maybe a paid vacation in San Francisco will appeal to her."

I had to laugh at that. "I think it just might."

Chapter 15

On Friday Aaron finally obtained from his friend
Rafael the exact location and a rough sketch of the
exterior and interior of the Sanders mansion. (At 16
rooms plus six bathrooms, it certainly qualified as a
mansion in my book.) According to Rafael, Chez
Sanders, as I was now thinking of it, was located on
several wooded acres near Los Altos, a short commute
down the Peninsula from San Francisco. That meant
our party could indeed be billeted in San Francisco,
with all the amenities that included. Although Aaron
didn't know the precise location of the violin in the
house, there was some kind of "art gallery" there,
which seemed like a logical place to display a rare
musical instrument. I congratulated Aaron on the
thoroughness of his research, and although it was
Rafael who had furnished the information to Aaron, he
gladly accepted the credit.

Aaron seemed to be mostly over whatever case of
nerves he'd had, and in fact he was like a small boy
embarking on his first day in school. He was an
effervescent mixture of enthusiasm for a new adventure
and dread of its unknown hazards. I impressed upon
him several times that this was, at bottom, a business
venture. It might succeed, and it might fail. Which
result obtained would depend on the thoroughness of
our planning, the precision of our actions, and a dollop

of dumb luck. I urged him to keep his emotions in check and to concentrate on business. To his credit, I'm sure Aaron did his best to comply, and I had high hopes that he would prove to be a competent cohort, or at least would not totally screw up the works.

****

Getting Sara to cooperate was another matter. It was partly that, although she enjoyed being on the fringe of my more exciting capers, she had assiduously stayed away from the epicenter, and this smacked too much of placing her squarely at ground zero. But there was also a more practical issue: She had several engagements that would have to be cancelled or rescheduled on short notice if she were to take off for a two-week dalliance with me and Aaron.

"I understand the problem," I told her as we shared evening coffee (there was no need for the wine this time). "And I'm sure we can get along without you. But I'd rather not. In addition to the fact that it would be fun to spend a couple of weeks in the Bay Area together, you're my safety net, and I'd hate to cross that high wire without one."

"I know, Flo, but it's such short notice. I can reschedule things like the two doctor's appointments, and I can cancel a meeting with my financial advisor. But you'll remember I told you about that guy I met at the library, and he's asked me out to a concert next Wednesday. I kind of hate to cancel a first date, if you know what I mean…" As I was well aware, to Sara having a good time was a high priority, and having a hot new boyfriend was the epitome of a good time.

"Sure, I understand," I said. "So let me sweeten the pot here. Aaron has lots of money and doesn't mind spending it. I'm sure he'll put us up at the Fairmont in San Francisco or whatever hotel we want, and the whole trip will be first class. Two weeks all-expenses-paid, like they say on the quiz shows, in the Bay Area. And as for this guy you met, if he can't wait a week or two to take you out, he probably isn't worth the trouble."

Sara thought about that while she sipped her coffee. As an attractive and "comfortably situated" single woman, she did not lack for romantic opportunities. And although this latest guy seemed a bit special, she knew I was right: If he couldn't handle a brief delay in what he no doubt saw as the first skirmish in a short campaign leading to Sara's bedroom, she was better off waiting for the next recruit.

"Okay, I'll go," she said at last. "It should be fun. And I'd hate to think of you out there in need of help with no one to call on, at least no one within a thousand miles or so."

"Great!" I leaned over and gave Sara a hug. "I'll tell Aaron everything's set. We'll all leave on Monday."

The next day, Saturday, I spent poring over the plan of Chez Sanders and considering the kinds of information I was still missing. Of course, one crucial question was how Aaron and I would get into the house in the first place, especially as it apparently was gated with a security guard on duty. This wouldn't be as simple as picking the lock on Donny Martin's front door, or getting into Aaron's room by impersonating a housekeeper.

Or would it?

Chapter 16

I didn't think I'd need to do a lot of packing. The tools I generally use for my housebreaking operations are very compact, so I can carry them in my pockets while on the job. The only "work clothes" I needed were as simple and as basic black as one could imagine. And I definitely would need an outfit or two for shopping, sightseeing, and dining. All work and no play....

As for Sara, she was treating this as almost exclusively a pleasure trip. She packed like a woman unconcerned about excess weight baggage fees, a woman of means who intended to make liberal use—on someone else's nickel, of course—of such luxuries as porters, taxi-drivers, and bellhops. If she didn't have to carry it, she told me, she didn't care what it weighed. Or cost.

Aaron, being a man, packed his tuxedo for the Los Angeles recitals together with two pairs of slacks, two pairs of jeans, some underwear, and a few mismatched shirts and was good to go. I hate that.

On Sunday morning our little trio was assembled in Aaron's suite and checked that we had all our essentials. Before we left, I excused myself to go back to my and Sara's room for something I'd forgotten. My real reason was to leave Aaron and Sara alone for a short while so they could talk and get a bit better acquainted. When I returned, we gathered our gear and headed for the airport, ready for adventure.

****

It was clear that Aaron liked Sara immediately, especially appreciating her cheerful demeanor, which seemed to lighten the atmosphere. I guess I was "all business" on what was, after all, a business trip; and Aaron was still excited and a bundle of nerves all at once. Sara, on the other hand, having accepted my characterization of the trip as a two-week all-expenses-paid holiday, was clearly determined to make the most of it.

As we arrived at the Alaska Airlines check-in, Sara looked around and asked Aaron, "Where's your violin? Aren't you going to L.A. for a recital or something?"

Aaron laughed. "You mean my priceless Guarneri?" He gave Sara a friendly wink. "I never take it on a plane with me. I shipped it ahead with a secure carrier. I'll pick it up when I arrive in L.A."

"Oh, I see. No, I guess I wouldn't trust the airline baggage handlers with it."

"Nor the overhead luggage compartment. I could have bought it a seat on the plane, but I'd rather not have to watch it constantly. No, this is a much less stressful way to go."

"Absolutely. But wait…you said it's not a real Guarneri, just a copy. So why…?"

Aaron laughed. "Because I have to treat it as if it is priceless, to maintain the illusion, which is the reason I bought the copy, right?"

I was glad Aaron was thinking of such details. I'm not sure that one would have occurred to me.

After a bit of small talk and hugs, we two girls and

Aaron entered the terminal separately, so as not to draw attention to the fact that we were traveling together. This was at my request, as I knew Aaron was a very recognizable celebrity, and in my line of work the less I'm noticed, the better. Besides, if we were going to pull off this job together, there could be a need down the line for each of us to deny we had ever even met the others.

I had managed to fit everything I needed into one medium-sized suitcase and a carry-on. Sara, on the other hand, who, as I mentioned, was unconcerned with weight restrictions, seemed to have packed for a world tour. A porter had carried her very large suitcase to the check-in counter, but when it came time to weigh it, she had trouble lifting it onto the scale. At first she was determined to manage by herself, but after two tries and a warning message from her back, her independent streak collapsed and she gratefully accepted my offer of help.

Aaron was a few places behind us in line, carrying only a small suitcase, a garment bag for his tux, and a day pack as a carry-on. He seemed to be smirking just a little at Sara's heavyweight dilemma. She stuck out her tongue at him just far enough to send a subtle message that only he would notice.

****

The flight to the Bay Area was uneventful, at least at the outset. Aaron had sprung for first class tickets, the first time either Sara or I had flown in anything but steerage. He had seated us together, with him behind. No one was in the seat next to him.

Seating was two abreast; and speaking of breasts, I couldn't help but notice Aaron staring at mine as I stretched to place my carry-on in the overhead compartment. He was not exactly leering, just politely appreciating the view. I didn't mind. I knew I was wearing a tight sweater; I knew I had a good figure, and to be honest, I probably would've been a bit disappointed if Aaron had been completely uninterested. I filed his reaction away for future reference.

During the flight, Aaron and I enjoyed several of the amenities of First Class, such as complimentary drinks, fluffy pillows, and a gourmet lunch; but we didn't enjoy them half as much as did Sara, who clearly thought this was the only way to fly. I had to discourage her from overindulging in food and beverages, assuring her that there would be plenty to eat and drink in San Francisco.

We were about halfway there when a stewardess distributed copies of the San Francisco Chronicle to anyone who wanted one. I accepted a newspaper and began casually perusing the pages.

Suddenly I gave a sharp intake of breath. I turned around and gestured frantically at Aaron. As we weren't supposed to be noticed as being together, he was no doubt surprised I would make such an obvious error of judgment and tried to ignore me. But when he saw the look on my face, he took the open newspaper I was handing him and looked at the place on the page to which I was pointing.

It went something like this:

UNEXPLAINED MURDER PROBED: Police in Redwood City reported finding the body of a man identified as Fredrick Ballard. Ballard, who had a long criminal record and had just recently been released from jail in Seattle, was found in a motel room in downtown Redwood City. He had been shot in the chest, apparently several days ago. Police are seeking clues to the assailant's motive, which apparently was not simple robbery, as Ballard's wallet, which contained over a hundred thousand dollars in cash, had not been taken. There appeared to have been a struggle before Ballard was killed. The murder weapon was not found.

According to police records, Ballard had shared an apartment in Seattle with a petty thief named Donny Martin. Martin was found shot to death in his apartment last week, and police speculate that whoever killed Martin may also have killed Ballard, but a motive has yet to be discovered. Our sources say one suspect in the Martin murder has been arrested, but no details were available.

All the article failed to add was the name of that prime suspect, a certain lady burglar.

I hurriedly unbuckled my seatbelt, stood up and slid in next to Aaron. Appearances would have to take second place to our need to discuss this new—and ugly—wrinkle in our plans.

"I guess that confirms what your friend Rafael told you," I said, "that Ballard had the violin and traded it for a shitload of money."

Aaron nodded.

"But then who killed him? Not your friend Rafael, I hope."

"Absolutely not," Aaron said quickly. "No chance. And besides, why would he give Ballard the money—which had to be that cash in his wallet—then kill him, but leave without taking the money back?"

"I guess you're right," I said. "But does that mean the same person who killed Martin killed Ballard? Or was Ballard killed in revenge for his killing Martin?"

"I have no idea. One thing's clear, though. This job keeps getting more dangerous by the minute."

Just then we hit an air pocket, the plane dipped, and, not having put on the seat belt, I was thrown to the side and against Aaron. He caught my arm and steadied me. The ride smoothed out, but he still held onto my hand.

"So maybe this guy Ballard comes back from prison," Aaron said after I had stabilized. He was looking a bit grave. "Martin shows him the violin or tells him about it and about Sanders, and Ballard decides he'll take the violin and make a deal for himself. He kills Martin in the process and heads south to deal with Sanders. Then someone kills Ballard, but apparently not for the violin, which had already been delivered to Sanders, or for the money in his wallet. If so, then we have no idea who killed Ballard, and Martin's killer is now dead and the chances of proving he did it have gotten a lot slimmer."

Which of course meant that the chances of proving I didn't kill Martin just got a lot slimmer as well.

"I guess one thing hasn't changed, though," Aaron continued. "The best chance we have of finding both my violin and proof that Martin was killed as part of a scheme to get it is at the home of the man who orchestrated that scheme."

Which of course was Chez Sanders.

****

We landed at San Francisco International and once off the plane made for the baggage carousel. I was walking with Sara, and suddenly I gripped her arm so tightly I probably cut off the circulation.

"What is it, Flo?" she asked, looking at me and seeing a bit of panic.

I relaxed my grip on her arm and took a deep breath.

"Nothing, nothing," I said once I'd composed myself. "I saw that police officer over there looking over the passengers, and suddenly I had this silly idea the police had found out I was leaving the state and were looking for me. It's hell being wanted for murder…"

"Don't be silly," Sara said. "You're not wanted for murder. And even if you are…I mean even if they think…oh, never mind. You'll be fine." And she turned and gave me a little hug, and I felt better. We were going to find out who killed Donny Martin, and then I'd put all this behind me. And it couldn't be too soon.

****

When all three of us had collected our luggage, we set out to find the car rental desks. Aaron was to rent a car, while Sara and I arrived at the hotel separately by taxi, again keeping our connection as invisible as possible. When we arrived at the hotel, likely at different times, we would check in separately.

Aaron stopped at a rental desk and Sara and I went on to the taxi stand. As Sara and I strolled along, I asked her whether she and Aaron had had a nice chat in his suite while I was gone.

"We did. He seems really nice, and down-to-earth, just like you said. Not what I would've expected from a big celebrity."

"So what did you talk about?"

96

For some reason, Sara seemed a little reluctant to answer that question, so I prompted further.

"Come on, you must've talked about something. The weather? His violin? Me?"

Sara looked at me a bit sheepishly. "As a matter of fact, yes."

"You talked about me?"

"Well, Aaron said he had a question he'd been wanting to ask me, being your best friend and all, and this was his chance. So I told him to go ahead and ask."

She certainly had my interest. "And what did he want to know?"

"He wanted to know how you happened to become a burglar. Sort of, 'What's a nice girl like her doing in a profession like that?'"

"Fair enough. And what did you tell him? That I thought it was safer than bank robbery and less messy than murder?"

Sara laughed. "Not exactly. I just told him the truth. That you'd always liked 'living on the edge' and taking risks, that you grew up poor, found yourself tempted by all the wonderful things you found while cleaning houses, and finally decided to acquire some for yourself. Like Robin Hood, but without the part about giving to the poor what you take from the rich."

"Hmm. So what did he say?"

"Not much. He didn't seem too judgmental. After all, he hired a burglar, which is almost the same as being one."

Then her tone changed a little. "To tell the truth, Flo, I think he really likes you, and he was glad to have a way to put your little, uh, peculiarity to one side."

"While still taking advantage of it, of course," I

said.

"Of course. He seems to be practical, as well as rich and famous and reasonably good looking."

Sara had that look in her eye, the "it's about time you hooked up with someone" look, and I didn't want any part of it. Not then, anyway.

"Don't get any ideas," I said. "This is strictly business, and any distractions can only screw up the mission we're on. And besides, famous violinists usually hook up with famous actresses or gorgeous models, not forty-something minor league burglars."

"Okay, okay," she said. "I'm just sayin'..."

"Well don't. But I'm glad he's satisfied with your explanation; it'll make everything a lot easier. So did you discuss anything other than me?"

"Well, after I told him about you, he wanted to know about me."

"What about you?"

"Why I'm still friends with you, knowing your...your profession."

"And what'd you say?"

"I first told him it was for the twenty-five percent cut of the loot you gave me, but when I saw he was taking me seriously and seemed kind of horrified, I told him the truth. You know, that we'd been close friends since school, and when you told me about your change of profession, I decided I'd rather remain friends than turn you in to the police. I pointed out we all have our little failings."

"Maybe not so little in my case, but you know how much I appreciate your sticking with me. Anything else?"

"He asked whether this was the first time I'd

actually participated in one of your…adventures."

"And you said…"

"And I said it was the first time I'd joined you willingly, and that I still didn't intend to get anywhere near the action. Just along for the ride."

I fervently hoped that ride wouldn't get too bumpy, for both our sakes.

****

As promised, Aaron had put us up at the ritzy Fairmont Hotel on Nob Hill. Again to avoid a direct connection between him and us, and to keep my name out of it as much as possible, Sara made the reservation in her name and paid for us both. Aaron had given each of us an advance to avoid our maxing out our credit cards. Mine, at least, maxes easily.

The Fairmont suited Sara and me just fine. The cable car ran by its door; the Mark Hopkins Hotel, with its famous Top of the Mark lounge, was across the street; and our suite had a killer view and all the comforts of home—someone else's home, of course, someone much wealthier than either of us.

The hotel consisted of its original, turn-of-the-century building and a modern tower. Our suite, 507, was on the fifth floor, while Aaron's was on the ninth, the top floor, both in the original wing. We girls and Aaron distributed ourselves in our allotted quarters and freshened up.

While I took a quick shower, Sara looked around, perusing the literature lying on the entrance table, including information about tourist attractions and the hotel itself.

When I'd finished my shower and dried off, I relinquished the bathroom to Sara.

"Did you know," Sara asked as she pulled off her sweater and bra, "this place was started before the 1906 earthquake? I mean, this very building."

"Really? Kind of gives you confidence it'll hold up at least as long as we'll be staying here."

"A lot more likely than some of the flimsy things they're putting up these days, I'll bet." And with that cynical observation, Sara stepped out of her skirt and panties and into the shower.

After everyone had had a chance to unpack and relax a bit, and Aaron had phoned to make sure Sara and I were "decent," he made his way down to the fifth floor and knocked on our door. It was opened by Sara.

With a perfectly straight face, Aaron asked, "Did someone here order a violinist?"

Sara turned around and called across the room to me, "Did we order a violinist?"

"No," I said, "I think it was a cellist. Room service is always getting them confused. But tell him to come in anyway and we'll make do."

Aaron laughed, as Sara stepped back to let him in.

"Sorry, they were all out of cellists and thought you wouldn't notice the difference," he said to me.

"Typical." Then getting down to business, I asked him, "When are you leaving for Los Angeles?"

"On Monday—tomorrow, that is. I have to be there for a rehearsal by three o'clock in the afternoon. The concerts are on Wednesday and Thursday. With luck, I'll be back here on Friday. Saturday at the latest."

I nodded and proceeded to outline my schedule for the same days.

"By the time you're back, we should be ready to make our final plans, based on what Sara and I learn during the week."

"Just so I don't end up having to put on a maid's uniform. My legs are not my most flattering feature."

I was tempted to say that indeed they were, but I decided Aaron might not take it as a joke, so I settled for, "We'll try to find you a more macho disguise if we can."

We toasted our future success with gin from the mini bar, and then we agreed to get together as soon as Aaron returned from Los Angeles. Satisfied things were in good hands, Aaron returned to his room to prepare for his flight in the morning.

When he had left, Sara asked me, "Did you ever get all of the details about the house and such that you asked Aaron for?"

"Well, mostly. I know the people he employs and I found a picture of Sanders, but it's from quite a while ago. I have a pretty good plan of the house. But what I don't have, and I wish I did, is exactly where that violin is being kept. Apparently Aaron's friend Rafael had no way of finding out without raising suspicion, since it's really none of his business. So we'll just play it by ear, I guess."

The pun was unintentional, and we both laughed. But when it came to burglary, I much would have preferred to be playing this violin from precisely written music.

****

Monday morning Aaron left for Los Angeles. Sara and I took the day to relax and do the "tourist thing," as Sara referred to it, not knowing just how much time we'd have for such activities once the Operation had begun in earnest. Starting out very early, we took both cable car lines from one end to the other. We visited Fisherman's Wharf (Sara bought a charm in the shape of a fish), Golden Gate Park (Sara bought a charm in the shape of a tree), Union Street (the Golden Gate Bridge), Chinatown (a Buddha), and the Zoo (a tiger). On the suggestion of my friend Lori, who had once lived in San Francisco, we took the outdoor glass elevator up the 32-story tower of the St Francis Hotel, overlooking Union Square. A few seconds after takeoff we found ourselves hanging out in space, soaring upward, with no apparent means of support. "Best free ride in the City," Lori had said, and I had to agree.

In the evening we chose from the hundreds of wonderful restaurants in the guidebook Sara had brought along, and we enjoyed a gourmet dinner, all on Aaron of course. We concluded our adventure with mai tais at the Hurricane Bar in the Fairmont's Tonga Room, laughing when caught in one of the periodic tropical rain storms that pass noisily through the restaurant each evening. We had to discourage half a dozen gentlemen from picking us up (much to Sara's regret), and we had to retire to bed much earlier than we would have liked; but even Sara realized we needed our beauty sleep.

We had a very full day ahead of us.

Chapter 17

The next morning Sara and I got up early and walked down the steep Mason Street hill toward Union Square, stopping at a small, friendly-looking car rental agency.

We had a short wait while the two desk clerks, one a woman of about fifty with a motherly smile and the other a man half her age with wavy black hair and a smile that was anything but motherly, served other customers.

"What kind of car are we getting?" Sara asked me in a low voice. "I hope it's a convertible."

"No convertible," I said, with emphasis on the "no."

Sara looked disappointed, her expression reminding me of a child whose mother has just refused to add a box of sugared cereal to the shopping cart.

To her credit, Sara didn't respond with either a tantrum or even "gee whiz," but she also didn't take my refusal as the final word.

"What've you got against a convertible? It's Aaron's nickel, and it'd make the trip more fun. How often can a person ride with the top down in Seattle?"

I sighed. I guess I knew when I asked Sara along I'd be dealing with this sort of issue. "I don't have anything against convertibles," I said, "but what we need is a car no one will notice, and one that will conceal us a bit, not advertise us. Two sexy ladies in an open Mustang will hardly blend into the landscape."

"No, I suppose not," Sara conceded.

"And while I understand about California and convertibles, I assume you've noticed that San Francisco generally has more fog than sun on a given day, so I don't think we're really missing anything. Now if we were in L.A...."

But that thought had to be suspended, because just then the two clerks became free almost simultaneously and it was our turn at the counter.

Predictably, I guess, I headed for the place in front of the motherly woman, and Sara for the one before the cute gentleman. Since I had the credit card and was in charge of the operation, Sara reluctantly acceded to my choice, but not without a meaningful exchange of smiles with the hunky clerk. I sighed again.

"A nice, comfortable, but plain car, please," I said when the woman behind the counter, who herself looked nice, comfortable, and plain, and whose name tag identified her as "Betty," inquired as to my wishes.

"What category of car would you like?" Betty asked. "Subcompact, compact, full-size, or one of our specialty vehicles like a Chevrolet Corvette or Dodge Grand Caravan? And we have a special this week on convertibles."

I really wished Betty hadn't said that, but it was too late. Sara looked like she was about to utter another plea for an open car, but I gave her a look that froze any plea in mid utter.

"Thanks, but we won't be needing anything that special. What do you have in a compact sedan?"

"Well, we have a nice Toyota Corolla…"

At this Sara took my arm and pulled me aside, asking Betty to excuse us for a few seconds.

"C'mon Flo, if we're gonna spend a lot of time in this car, let's at least get one that's comfortable and roomy. We're not trying to save money here."

This time I had to agree. I knew we had a long day (or days) of surveillance ahead, and we needed a comfortable car in which to do it. And after turning down the convertible, I suppose I owed Sara this one anyway.

"You're right. Let's get something a little more luxurious. No Corolla."

Sara released my arm, and I returned to the spot in front of Betty.

"What full-size cars do you have?"

"I think we have a very nice Buick LaCross," Betty said, looking at her computer screen. "Dark blue."

Sara's ears perked up, as she herself owned a Buick. Any resemblance between that iron monster and a modern Buick, however, was akin to that between a Model T and a Mustang.

"For how long will you want it?" Betty asked.

I thought about this. I wasn't sure, but better to be safe.

"Let's say one week."

Betty consulted the computer screen again. "It's only $634.46 a week, and that includes unlimited mileage."

Although I would never pay so much to rent a car on my own, I felt no qualms about spending Aaron's money lavishly, as he had insisted we were free to do. And it was, after all, in the name of more effective surveillance.

"Sounds fine," I said to Betty. "Okay with you, Sara?"

"Yes, fine," Sara replied. She apparently had gotten over the loss of her convertible, at least for the time being.

I handed the woman my credit card—no, not with my real name on it, as my recent run-in with the law probably would show up on their computer with a big red flag—but one of the "extras" I keep for special occasions like this—and we were the proud, if temporary, possessors of a large blue Buick.

We stopped at a grocery for some snack foods and a newsstand for an assortment of magazines and at a high-tech shop so I could pick up an item or two. Then we returned to the hotel, packed up a few odds and ends, and departed in our Buick, a vehicle of substantial proportions and living room comfort, me at the wheel and Sara riding shotgun, on our way south.

We drove in contented silence the forty miles down the Peninsula into the heart of Silicon Valley. Following the directions Betty had given me at the rental office, I took Highway 101, the Bayshore Freeway. It was fast, but it was ugly, miles of barren concrete plastered over what doubtless had once been open fields and orchards. Less than an hour later, we arrived at our destination, the little upscale community of Los Altos.

It was a pleasantly warm day, and we had a leisurely lunch on Main Street. I had noticed Sara flirting with two men at the next table and had to remind her that we had work to do later. After lunch we strolled down Main Street, enjoying the village atmosphere. The many shops and boutiques made for interesting window shopping, and in a small drug store I purchased a map of the town and surrounding area. We bought ice cream cones at a cute little sweets shop and sat on a shady bench while I located our target on the map. When we returned to the car, I programmed the address into the GPS that had come with the Buick. I then handed the map to Sara.

"Why did you buy this if you were going to use the GPS?" Sara asked.

"Because I don't trust these things. I always like to have a paper map to check against what the little voice in the box tells me to do."

"I've never used one," Sara said. "Why don't you trust them?"

"Well, for one thing, the voice in these things is always so smarmy and superior-sounding, I'm tempted to do the opposite of what she tells me, just to spite her. I mean, just because she knows the way to every damn address in the world, while I can't remember how to get to the dealer to take my car in twice a year…"

"I know what you mean," Sara sympathized. "I'm terrible with directions."

"Just the quality we want in our navigator. But the real reason I don't trust the little voice is that the first time I used one of these things," I said, pointing to the screen, "which I rented with a car in L.A., it missed the target by two blocks, took me up a blind alley, and mistook the off-ramp of the Santa Monica Freeway for the onramp to the San Diego Freeway."

"It must have been a lemon," Sara suggested.

"Yeah, but I was the one that almost got squished into lemonade. And I've read about people following GPS directions into swamps, off uncompleted overpasses, and the wrong way down one-way streets. So now I always like to have a map and, if possible, a live backup navigator. Even one who has no sense of direction."

"That's me," Sara laughed and punched "Go" on the GPS.

With the "little voice" calling out directions, and Sara checking them on the local map, we headed for La Paloma Road. I had done my best to check out the landscape online before we left the hotel, but what I'd mostly seen was the tops of the tall trees that dominated the landscape. The only way to find out what lay beneath that canopy was by personal observation.

We soon found ourselves on a narrow country lane about two miles outside of town. (According to the little voice in the black box, we were on "Lapaloma Road," one word, the first part rhyming with "Napa," which made me grind my teeth.) On both sides of the road were large estates, grand homes flanked by green pastures and surrounded by white post-and-rail fences. Most had a barn or stable nearby, and here and there a horse or two could be seen grazing lazily. Periodically there were stands of tall trees, mostly fir, cedar, or eucalyptus, partially obscuring the view and casting dappled shadows across the narrow strip of blacktop.

"Not a bad place to live," Sara commented as she gazed from one bucolic scene to another.

"I suppose, if that's the lifestyle you prefer," I said. "Not enough excitement for me, not enough action, unless you count the occasional high-stakes horseshoe tournament."

"Oh, I'm sure there's more excitement than that," Sara said. "But I get your point. A little too leisurely for you, and probably for me, too. But I have a feeling what we've come here to do won't be leisurely at all, and will involve more than enough excitement."

"Yeah," I agreed, "and it starts now. There's the house, on the right."

I pulled the car over by the left side of the road and parked in front of what looked like a small public park, elevated from the road. There were a few swings and picnic benches, and its several tall trees cast a welcome pool of shade onto our parked car and the rest of the road.

I got out a pair of binoculars and directed them toward the house across the road.

"It looks like you enter from this road, but there's a gate farther up, and I can see some people around it. That must be the security point. Let's see if there's any other way in."

We checked around the property, but there didn't seem to be another way in. There also didn't seem to be any stores or gas stations in this rural area.

"In a job like this, it's important to know where the nearest public rest room is," I said. "Doesn't look like there is one here."

"That's okay," Sara said. "I saw restrooms at that little park we parked near."

"Good. It sure beats going behind a tree."

"Funny how in the movies no one ever seems to have that problem," Sara said. "Maybe that's because men write most of the scripts."

I drove up the driveway to the little park and stopped the car.

"Now comes the boring part," I told Sara. "Watching that entrance, to see who comes in and who goes out, and when."

"Won't they see the car hanging around and think it's suspicious?"

"That's assuming they see us. I don't think they will, at least not from the house. So we can stay here pretty much all day if we have to."

"You mean we're going to sit here all day just watching the house? What happened to the vacation in San Francisco?"

"Hey," I said, "we have to earn our keep, don't we? But I understand why you'd rather not spend your time out here. I guess I just wanted company. Tomorrow I can drive down by myself and you can stay in the city and play."

Sara was silent, and she let the matter rest. I knew how to inject a subtle bit of guilt into an otherwise reasonable-sounding statement.

Nothing of note happened for the next hour or so, and as it was by now getting late in the afternoon, I decided to drive back to San Francisco before we became stuck in the notorious rush hour commute traffic.

Tomorrow would be our first full day observing Chez Sanders.

Chapter 18

The next day, Wednesday, I was up just after dawn. Definitely not a time of day I'm used to seeing. I wanted to be on the job, and to be parked in close proximity to Sanders' house, by 8 a.m., so as not to miss any important activity there.

I made my way to the window of our Fairmont suite and drew back the curtains.

What I saw was fog. If San Francisco is famous for anything other than its hills, its restaurants, its cable cars, and its cost of living, it probably is its fog. Spend a few days here, and you find out why. Even on days that promise to be bright and sunny from noon to dusk, more often than not a dense fog rolls in at night, curling itself up comfortably against those seven hills and filling with moist droplets every open space between them. San Franciscans I've met seem to either love it or hate it, and those in the latter group generally leave the city for its sunnier suburbs at their first opportunity.

It occurred to me as I stared out the window that fog might be a good thing for a burglar. Working at night in a dark house has its advantages, of course, especially if the owners of the premises are asleep or not at home. But a dark interior makes it difficult to see and get around inside, and a flashlight might be noticed from the outside. The fog outside our window, however, was almost as impenetrable as night, if not more so; no one out on the street could see in, just as I couldn't see out. Yet the fog let in enough light that I could see around the room perfectly well. A nice, natural opaque curtain behind which to operate. Maybe I'd have to come down for a working holiday sometime.

But I was wasting time with these reveries. There was work to be done.

****

Sara and I were sharing a large and comfortable suite, certainly larger and more comfortable than either of us had ever stayed in before. I was sleeping in the bedroom and Sara in the living room area on a luxurious sofa bed. While I padded sleepily into the bathroom to shower and dress, Sara awoke and sat up. She looked my way, stretched lazily, and lay back down, eyes open, apparently trying to orient herself to her strange surroundings. I let her lie there and figure it out while I did my ablutions.

When I came out of the bathroom, I looked over at Sara. Still horizontal and cozy.

"What?" Apparently Sara had detected a note of reproof in my eyes.

"Nothing. I hope I didn't wake you up. I tried to be as quiet as possible."

"No, you didn't wake me. I'm always awake at six a.m. Early to bed, early to rise, and all that." Yeah, sure.

"Well, go back to sleep. I'll be outta here pretty soon."

Rather than closing her eyes, however, Sara sat back up. Slowly and dramatically, like a magician revealing the soundness of the woman he had just sawed in half, she drew back the green-and-gold duvet with which she had been covered. It revealed only that she was wearing a skimpy nightie that had managed to work its way up past her navel. She swung her legs out of bed and the rest of her followed. She stood up and smoothed out her nightie as she slipped into her pink backless travel slippers.

"Where're you going?" I asked.

"Where d'ya think?" she answered through a yawn, still sounding more asleep than awake.

"To the bathroom?" It seemed like a logical guess.

"Well, yeah; but then I'm coming with you. On your stakeout thingy." Another yawn.

"Are you sure? You didn't seem too enthusiastic yesterday, and I really do understand."

"Sure I'm sure. Hey, a good night's sleep can be vastly overrated; and besides, how would I feel if you ended up having all the fun out there while I was boring myself with stuff like museums and cable cars and fancy restaurants?" She headed for the bathroom, her path meandering a bit as she yawned and stretched.

I have to admit I was very pleased. I'd assumed I would be heading for Los Altos alone.

"Okay, that's great," I said to Sara's back as the bathroom door was closing. "I really do appreciate the company. And I'm sure we'll have more chances to see the sights after we get the lay of the land down in Los Altos."

But I'm sure Sara didn't hear the last few words. She was already standing under a cold shower, apparently the only thing that was going to render her sufficiently awake to make good on her rash decision to ride along on her friend's return to Chez Sanders.

****

We made our way out of the city. Sara seemed sufficiently awake by now and in fact seemed to be enjoying the ride, seeing the city wake up and begin to stir beneath its foggy overcoat.

"So how long are we gonna be watching this place before you and Aaron are ready to do your thing?" she asked.

"Oh, two days should be sufficient," I assured her. I didn't mention that it could as easily be four or five.

Sara yawned. She looked over at me, then said, "Hey, where'd you get the fancy watch? It's new, isn't it?"

I smiled and glanced at my wrist and the small but stylish instrument I was wearing. "Picked it up in that store we stopped at yesterday. Let's just say Aaron bought me a nice present, even if he doesn't know it yet."

"But you already had a nice watch—maybe not as fancy, but it told the time."

"I know. But this isn't just a watch. I have no idea what we'll run into on this job, or how I'll get the evidence of who killed Martin, so I decided it was time to go high-tech. This little baby is a top-of-the-line smartwatch. If it'll do everything they told me it will, compared to it my smartphone is merely reasonably intelligent."

"Yeah, well next time, maybe he could buy us both one."

"I'll be sure to tell him," I said. And with that Sara lapsed back into sightseeing and silence.

We were in Los Altos in just under an hour and headed straight for La Paloma Road. I drove to the little park we had seen the day before, across the road from

Chez Sanders. We again parked under the trees in the park, which we learned from a sign at the entrance was called Joseph Hyde Park. Not exactly the Hyde Park in London; we dubbed it Little Hyde Park. No one else was about and the silence was deafening. From between the tall trees we could clearly see the entrance to the Sanders driveway.

I got out my binoculars, while Sara chose a magazine from a stack she had bought at the hotel newsstand. Provisioned with beverages by Starbucks and serenaded by music from the local classical station, we settled in.

Eight a.m. passed, as did nine and ten, and the only activity we observed on the Sanders driveway was a black Mercedes sedan, probably carrying Sanders himself, leaving the house at 8:50; a U.P.S. delivery truck entering at 9:15 and leaving again five minutes later; and two modest passenger cars with lone male drivers entering the driveway at 8:55 and 9:05 respectively.

"I wonder who it is visiting Sanders' house," Sara said. "D'ya think he's really the kingpin of some big smuggling ring and only uses the grocery business as a front? Maybe those were two of his henchmen reporting for work. Maybe—"

"Maybe we shouldn't let our imagination get away from us," I said before Sara could conjure up any deeper mysteries.

Sara sighed. "I guess you're right. But it would be a lot more exciting if I were right."

"Don't worry. I have a feeling things will get exciting enough without adding the Sopranos to the mix."

And it wasn't a good feeling.

****

At 9:50, one of the cars carrying a lone driver departed, and twenty minutes later the other did likewise. What their business there had been was still a mystery. Was one of them the killer of Fred Ballard? Or of Donny Martin? Or was I the one letting my imagination run away this time?

About this time Sara stretched and yawned. "I don't want to complain," she complained, "but everything from my neck to my butt is stiff, and if I don't move around a bit soon, I may end up permanently frozen in sitting position."

"Well, we should move on anyway," I said, also stretching and moving my head up and down to loosen up my neck muscles. "We don't want to become too obvious in case anyone notices we've been here all morning." While Sara was searching for something in her purse, I put the binoculars down and reached forward to start the engine. That's when we heard a knock on the driver's side window.

Startled, Sara and I both looked to the left. Standing next to the car and peering in through dark aviator-style sunglasses was a tall man in a light blue shirt. On the shirt was a bronze-colored badge in the shape of a star. I glanced into the rear-view mirror and there, sure enough, was a car with a light bar across its roof. I lowered the window, both nervous about what the officer might want and curious about the same thing.

"Yes, officer? Surely I wasn't speeding."

The man with the badge smiled. "No, ma'am. Just the opposite. I couldn't help noticing that you've been parked here since early this morning, and I just thought I'd check to see if you needed any…assistance."

I shifted into all-innocence mode, while inwardly berating myself for making us conspicuous by staying too long in one place.

"Why no, officer," I said, "we're just fine. Been driving all night and stopped here to rest a bit. I guess we must have fallen asleep for a while."

While I said this, the officer's eyes swept the inside of the car. They reached and focused on the binoculars lying next to me.

"Could I ask what the binoculars are for? Not a lot to look at out here."

Oh great, now he suspects us of spying on someone, which of course is exactly what we're doing, dammit. But to the officer I merely said, "Oh, we always carry these when we travel. We're both bird watchers, and one of the great things about visiting new places is getting to see the different species that live there. Just this morning I spotted a red-throated chickadee that I'd never seen before." As I wouldn't know a chickadee from a bald eagle, I fervently hoped I had not encountered the one officer on the Los Altos police force who was a serious birder. Meanwhile, next to me, Sara nodded vigorously, doing her best to hold up her part of the charade.

The officer seemed to consider my explanation for a minute before accepting it, which apparently he did. Either that or he couldn't think of any crime connected with extended parking or possession of a pair of binoculars. With a polite "Thank you, ma'am," an admonition to make sure we were fully awake before driving on, and a nod to Sara, he returned to his car. He backed up and left us sitting there, drenched in perspiration, and not from the temperature.

"That was close," Sara said after a few moments of silence. "But I guess no harm done. Good thinking about the bird watching."

I was not so sanguine. "The harm is that a police officer now has seen us hanging around this area. Not only will we have to be careful to avoid running into him again, but if a crime should be reported at the Sanders house in the next few days, we just might be high on the list of suspicious characters."

"At least he didn't ask for our identification," Sara said. "He doesn't know our names."

"No, but he probably noted down our license number, which would lead to the rental agency and then to us. Let's get out of here."

I started the engine and eased the car out of the roadside park. At the exit, I turned toward town.

"Are we through here for the day?" Sara asked hopefully.

"Not at all. We just have to rent a different car. As different as possible. This one's been compromised." I guess I didn't sound pleased, because Sara didn't take the opportunity to ask whether this time we could get a convertible.

****

We didn't drive all the way back to San Francisco to change cars. I merely parked the Buick on the street near the local car rental office (it seemed to be the only one in town, and unfortunately the same company as we rented the Buick from) and there we rented a plain-vanilla Dodge minivan, very far in appearance, and most other features, from the Buick, and even farther from Sara's preferred convertible. This one went out in Sara's name, since the company might frown on one person renting two cars simultaneously in two different locations.

Once again we drove out to La Paloma Road and Little Hyde Park. We sat down on a picnic bench, enjoying the shade and the breeze, and continued to watch the road, this time without binoculars. Occasionally we got up and walked around to stretch our legs. In a car or on foot, this was, as I had expected, a very boring job. I wondered how much longer Sara would put up with it.

"Flo," Sara asked at about two o'clock, "I guess I should've asked this a long time ago, but what exactly is it we're looking for? That is, are we keeping track of who comes and goes just to get an idea of the traffic, or are we waiting for something, or somebody, specific?"

"Well, a little of both," I said. "We do need to know how busy the traffic is, as you put it, so we'll know if we're likely to be dealing with a lot of people and interruptions while we, uh, work. But mostly I'm hoping we find that Sanders, like most people with money and big houses these days, employs a cleaning crew of some sort that comes on a regular basis, just like I used to do in my former life. And if he does have a maid service, when the time comes I hope I can do the same thing I did at Aaron's hotel: become one of the maids."

"That's fine for you, I guess, but somehow I can't picture Aaron as a housemaid, and you already assured him he wouldn't have to dress in a maid's uniform."

"Yeah, I know," I said a bit irritably. "I haven't figured that part out yet."

Sara rolled her eyes at this, but she said nothing. It was my profession, my plan—and my funeral if it didn't work. She was just along for the ride—and the wait.

Chapter 19

It wasn't until the next morning that we finally hit pay dirt. The previous evening, we had turned in the minivan at the Los Altos rental office, picked up the Buick, and back in San Francisco had exchanged it for a white BMW, one of the rental agency's most expensive selections. Although the minivan had not been "compromised" like the Buick, I wanted to avoid any chance that someone would notice that the same car was parked by the Sanders house two days in a row. Again, the cars were as different as they could be.

Sara made one last plea for a convertible—I was beginning to think it was some kind of obsession with her. Maybe it was.

"If you want it to be as different from the last two as possible, then let's go all the way," Sara cajoled. And this time, I gave in. Sara had a good point, and it couldn't hurt to drive an open car down the freeway.

"But once we get near the Sanders house," I said, "the top goes up, so we aren't recognizable to anyone seeing the car. Agreed?"

Sara readily agreed.

The ubiquitous fog having burned off early, it was just warm enough to enjoy top-down driving. Sara wore a wide-brim straw hat, held on by a pink ribbon under her chin, and the smile never left her face during the entire drive. I had to admit that, all things being equal, an open-air white BMW was definitely the way to go. A person could get used to this.

But eventually pleasure ended and work began again. We arrived at Little Hyde Park just after 8:00 a.m. Heavy traffic had caused us to be a bit later than I'd wanted. We drove in and parked under the same tree as the day before.

Sara had her magazines at the ready, together with a supply of snacks, and I had my binoculars out. But before either of us had settled in for another long vigil, the security guard arrived at the Sanders house in a blue Honda decorated with a yellow light bar, parking next to the security gate. And several minutes later a white Ford Explorer appeared around the bend in La Paloma Road. It paused across from the driveway entrance, its turn signal blinking, to let a refuse truck pass, which gave me enough time to read the sign on the door of the car: "TidyHome Maid Service." There was a phone number, but no address. I dictated and Sara, having grabbed the pad and pen she had brought along, wrote down the sign's message. It was exactly 8:15 a.m.

"I can see two people in the car," I reported, "and what looks like cleaning supplies in the back seat."

As soon as the truck had passed, the Explorer made the turn into the driveway and disappeared into the fog. I was sorry I couldn't see its arrival at the house, because I wanted to know to which side of the house—front or back entrance—it went.

"That's the one I've been waiting for," I said with satisfaction.

"You mean we can leave now?" Sara asked, perhaps sounding a bit too hopeful.

"Yes, I think so. We aren't going to learn much

more sitting here, especially through the fog."

On the way back to San Francisco, Sara said, "I forget what Aaron said about whether this Sanders guy is married. Is there a Mrs. Sanders who stays home all day?"

"No, according to the bio I read online, there isn't. Once Sanders leaves for the day, there should only be employees left at the house. They should be easier to deal with than the owner's wife would be."

"Did Aaron's friend say anything about who those employees might be? And is he one of them?"

"Well, not exactly. See, he doesn't live at the house, although he's there frequently on Sanders' business. All he said was that there's a housekeeper, who lives in, and a chauffeur, who also lives there and who's around the house doing odd jobs when he isn't driving Sanders somewhere. And of course we've seen there's a guard at the gate."

"Doesn't sound too bad," Sara said.

"Hmm" was all I responded. That kinda depends whether you're the burglar.

****

When we arrived back at the hotel, Sara headed for the bathroom and soon stood naked under a hot shower, finally able to relax a bit. Meanwhile I sat at the round walnut table and pored over note pads filled with diagrams, lists, and hypothetical scenarios, several of which were ostentatiously crossed out.

Where was the violin now? Was it in that "gallery" Rafael had mentioned? I thought it very possible, as Sanders probably would want to display his new prize, at least to a select few friends, and at least until he swapped it for Suzuki's Monet. But then, once Aaron and I were in the house (and that itself, of course, was a major undertaking), how would we gain entry to that room?

On a different but related note, would we encounter Donny Martin's killer at Chez Sanders? Or Fred Ballard's? Or both? And how would we know them?

Then there was the question of Aaron's role in the drama. As he had insisted on having one, and an active one at that, for better or worse he would be on the scene with me. And since I could hardly trust him, as a newbie, to act on his own, his role would have to mirror mine; in other words, wherever I would be going, Aaron would be found as well. For perhaps the hundredth time in the past several weeks, I asked myself what had possessed me to agree to Aaron's harebrained proposal. Was it, as Sara had earlier hinted, something personal about Aaron? If so, it would be a very unprofessional, and therefore very dangerous, motivation. I dismissed the idea as absurd.

By the time I had added most of our new information into my old plans, it was time for dinner, and I decided I could finish my work later in the evening. Fortunately, reconnaissance in Los Altos was virtually completed. Sara and I would now have a day or two to rest in San Francisco while we waited for Aaron to return from Los Angeles.

On our own in San Francisco, on someone else's credit card.

I felt better already.

Chapter 20

"So what's on for tonight?" Sara asked as she and I relaxed in our suite. Her shower and dinner had revived her and she was feeling restless. We had dined elegantly once again in the hotel's Tonga Room, complete with mai tai cocktails topped by little paper umbrellas, and accompanied by another indoor tropical storm.

"I'm afraid I'm just too tired to go out," I told Sara. It wasn't what she wanted to hear.

"But geez, Flo, how often are we gonna be in San Francisco? And with someone else's credit card, too?"

"I know, Sara, and I wish I could party, but I'm here on business. But you're not, so don't let me stop you."

Sara thought about that for a minute.

"Well...I suppose I could go out by myself for a while. The Mark Hopkins is just across the street, and I've wanted to get to the Top of the Mark; I could go over and have a cocktail or two. Maybe find someone interesting to talk to."

"Sure," I agreed enthusiastically. I was feeling a bit guilty about dragging Sara into the boring stakeout the last few days. "Just remember that Aaron might be back sometime tomorrow, so we have to be ready to move on to the next stage in our plans. Don't overdo."

Sara gave me her most innocent, injured look.

"*Moi*? What makes you think I would overdo anything?"

I rolled my eyes slightly and replied, "What indeed. Let's just say you and alcohol have a love-hate relationship—you love to take a drink or two, and when you go beyond that you always hate yourself in the morning. So I repeat, don't overdo."

Sara's rueful smile could best be translated: "When you're right, you're right."

All she said was, "Yes, ma'am."

Sara quickly changed into a slinky black cocktail dress, threw on her coat, and with a flourish left me to my planning. Sitting in my hotel-supplied plush robe in one of the suite's overstuffed chairs, I would've liked to go along, but I was tired and a hot bath and a TV movie appealed to me even more.

****

As the evening progressed, I started to become a little concerned that Sara hadn't returned or even phoned. I had assumed she would have her two drinks at the Top of the Mark and make her way home, taking an hour or two at the most. But by midnight she was still not back, and I was genuinely worried.

I called Sara's cell number, but apparently she had turned off her phone. I considered calling the police, but that had the potential of complicating our mission. Finally I decided to go to bed and deal with Sara in the morning. She was a big girl and could take care of herself.

Or so I hoped.

****

At 7:30 the next morning, the phone next to my bed rang. It woke me out of a deep sleep, but as soon as

I was awake I remembered Sara was still unaccounted for—I glanced at her bed and saw it hadn't been slept in—and began to panic. How could I wait this long to do something to locate Sara? It was the fourth ring before I finally answered the phone.

"Hello," I said in a voice that I'm sure sounded somewhere between frantic and pissed off.

"Flo, it's Sara."

Exhale. "Where the hell are you? I've been really worried. Why didn't you come home last night?"

"I'm really sorry, Flo. I guess I had a little too much to drink and ended up spending the night over here at the Mark."

"You mean you were too drunk to make it across the street?"

"Well…not exactly. I spent the night with someone."

I might've known. There were a few seconds of silence, during which I counted to ten, before I said, "With someone. A male someone?"

"Yes."

"I see. Well, that part's none of my business, I guess, but I sure as hell wish you'd have been sober enough to at least call. I was so worried I was ready to call the police, and you know for me that's gotta be the very last resort!"

"I know, and I'm sorry. Anyway, I'll be over there as soon as…"

Apparently whoever she had spent the night with was still there and probably caressing some very sensitive area of her body, because I could hear a sigh and a soft giggle before Sara continued: "As soon as I take care of something here. And it won't happen again,

I promise."

I just sighed. "Well, I'm glad you're okay. Don't be too long—we've still got work to do."

"I won't," Sara assured me. "Bye."

****

When Sara finally arrived back at the suite, about an hour later, I sat her down and insisted she tell me just how she happened to end up in some strange bed for the night. I mean, a part of me didn't really want to know, but another part wanted every detail.

Sara sighed and sat back on the sofa, sipping a cup of coffee, and told her sad story.

"Well, if you want all the details, I took the elevator down to the lobby and crossed to the hotel entrance. There the doorman opened one of the glass doors for me and inquired whether I needed a cab.

"I said no, I'm just crossing the street.

"The doorman saluted politely, crossed the sidewalk and pressed the button for a 'walk' signal. At the front door of the Mark Hopkins, another doorman opened the door and ushered me in.

"I could get used to this, I thought. So I entered the elevator and pressed the highest button for the bar at the Top of the Mark.

"And that's when things began to get a bit crazy."

Chapter 21

"When I woke up this morning," Sara said, "I was immediately aware that something was wrong. Not necessarily wrong in a bad way, but definitely wrong.

"To begin with, I wasn't in my own bed. That by itself wasn't surprising, of course, since I remembered I was in San Francisco, not Seattle. Looking around the room, I was definitely in an elegant hotel suite. The only problem was that it wasn't the suite, or the bed, I'd slept in the night before. It was even more elegant than the one here at the Fairmont; but it was still the wrong one."

The second problem, Sara said, was that she was not alone, and her bedmate was not me. "Sleeping next to me in this king-size bed was definitely a man. A good-looking man, at that. He was covered by a sheet, which I gently lifted to get a better view. The guy was perhaps 40 years old, well-groomed, short-cropped hair with a hint of gray, ripped abs, and...*geez,* I thought, *this guy's naked!*

"Worse yet, so was I. I suddenly realized that I was wearing no nightie, no bra, no panties...no anything."

Shit! I'd been right. She clearly had overdone!

"I guess my first impulse was to pull the sheet up to cover myself. But of course that was a bit silly: whatever had happened between the time I entered the elevator and that moment, it obviously had involved my naked body in a way that would make next-morning modesty almost hypocritical."

As I listened to Sara's story, I couldn't help wondering how I would have reacted if I woke up naked in an elegant suite next to a similarly-attired strange man. But I didn't have that kind of luck.

Sara continued: "My head was really throbbing from what must've been far too many cocktails, but I slowly began to recall some of the events between pressing that top button in the elevator and waking up in that strange bed. The name Roger seemed to come to me. And he was some kind of big shot, the CEO of…of some company I can't remember the name of. Well-heeled. I'd had a cocktail or two alone, then an innocent little flirtation with this man down the bar, then some quiet conversation—about what I don't remember—and a few more cocktails…that, I guess, was when I overdid it…and finally an invitation to continue the conversation in his suite. So that's where I imagined I must be. And from the look of it, Roger Whatever-his-name-was didn't lie to me; that suite had to cost six, maybe seven hundred a night if it cost a dime."

Well, at least she didn't surrender her virtue cheaply.

Of course, "virtue" might be the wrong word here. While she was not what you'd call promiscuous, Sara was by no means a virgin, and under the right circumstances she enjoyed a romp in the hay as much as the next woman—maybe more. So I'm sure the fact that she probably had had sex with this man was not in itself a huge deal for her. But I'm also sure she was used to having sex with men she knew well, in surroundings with which she was familiar, and while she was fully conscious. *My God, she doesn't even know if she had a good time!*

"Anyway, about the time I was remembering some of the details," Sara went on, "the body next to me moved. I looked over and saw it open one eye, then the other, and a smile broke out on its face. It wasn't a smile of triumph, just a kind of warm smile of contentment.

"He said, 'Hey, honeybunch. Glad you're still here.' He had a slight Southern accent, like someone who was born in the South but had lived in Yankee country since he was a kid.

"I honestly didn't know how to respond. I guess I smiled, and then I decided I had neither the energy nor the desire to play it coy, so I confessed. I said, 'I'm sorry, but I must've had a lot to drink, because I don't remember much about how I got here or what happened afterwards.'

"Roger—turned out I'd remembered his name correctly—kind of patted my...well, patted me and said, 'Well, now, I can assure you that you had a wonderful time. I know I did.' Then he said we'd met upstairs in the bar, had a few drinks, talked a little, then we came down there to his place and, well, one thing kinda led to another, and...and there we were."

I said, 'Yes, I see that. And, uh, did you..."

"Have sex? Funny, I asked him that too."

"And what did he say?" I was sure this was not a common question for a guy to be asked, especially after waking up with a naked woman in his bed.

"He said, 'Absolutely!' And that we both enjoyed ourselves immensely. And then he kind of began doing some nice things to my body and I was about to find out if he was right about that, when I sat bolt upright and asked Roger the time.

"It was 7:30 already! I said, 'My friend will think I've been kidnapped or run over or I don't know what! I've got to call her!' He was very understanding. I was so frantic I couldn't think how to get the Fairmont's number. He told me just to call the operator and ask her for it. I almost couldn't find the '0' on the phone I was in such a state. Fortunately the operator not only gave me the number but even dialed it for me."

I thought about that for a moment. She had called at 7:30, but she hadn't arrived back here until about 8:30. "So why did it take you so long to get here once we'd spoken?"

Sara looked distinctly sheepish. "Well, once I'd assured you I was okay, there didn't seem to be any hurry, and, well, Roger was making these nice…"

"Never mind. I get the picture. Spare me the erotic details," I said. I could understand Sara wanting to have some fun while in the city, even fun of the carnal variety. I myself hadn't been in bed with a man in quite a while, preoccupied as I was with establishing my new profession. In fact, Sara had occasionally accused me, in a good-natured way, of being far too "uptight," too inhibited when it came to men; and perhaps there was some truth in that. I've passed up a few opportunities for, shall we say, intimacy, that Sara, not to mention most unattached women my age, would have had no trouble accepting. And whatever my inclinations might be at other times, when I'm on the job, as I now was, I had to maintain a strict separation between work and play. But I also had to remember that Sara had come along as a companion, not an accomplice. I couldn't expect the same discipline of her as I demanded of myself.

I changed the subject, at least slightly: "Tell me more about this Roger."

"Well, his last name is Andrews. He has to be rich, because you should see his suite. It has spectacular views of Alcatraz, the Golden Gate Bridge, everything. And geez, the bathroom—which also looks out on Alcatraz—is almost as large as my entire apartment at home, and far more elegant."

"So are you planning to see the guy again?"

"We did exchange contact information. And he seemed really concerned about how I felt. About the night before, I mean."

"What do you mean, concerned?"

"He said, 'I don't want you to think I'm the kind of guy who takes advantage of a helpless woman. Honest, you were acting like you knew exactly what you were doing; that is, what we were doing.'"

Sara laughed. "I'm sure I did, at the time. The problem is, of course, as I told him, when I have too much to drink, I don't necessarily lose control of my actions—although that's certainly possible—but the next day I can't remember much of what happened. So I said I didn't feel violated or anything like that."

"And what did he say to that?"

"He said, 'That's good, because I remember everything that happened, and it was all good. And I hope we can see each other again sometime.' Apparently he lives in L.A.. He asked if I get down this way very often. I said no, this was my first trip to San Francisco, and I've only been to Los Angeles once, several years ago.

"Then he asked me whether I was here on business or pleasure. I wasn't sure how to answer that. I think I said, 'Well, up until last night it was business.' And then I had this horrible thought that maybe I had, you know, told him what our 'business' here was."

Which is exactly the horrible thought I had just had myself. Had Sara gone and blown our cover? And to a stranger?

"And had you?"

"Apparently not. At least Roger said I didn't mention anything about why I was in San Francisco. He said I just told him I was down here with a friend and staying at the Fairmont, helping my friend out with her business.

"He said he has a few clients down the Peninsula, so maybe we'll run into each other somewhere."

"I sure hope it's not in Los Altos," I said. "If you do, don't introduce him to me, please. So what business is your Roger in that takes him up and down the state?"

"He's not 'my Roger,' and I'm not completely sure. I remember he said he was the CEO of some big corporation, but when I asked him what the company did, he sort of hesitated and said it was 'a bit complicated,' but that he was in some kind of 'import/export business.' They're apparently based in L.A. and have offices in New York and a few foreign countries."

"Hmm. I guess no harm was done," I said, fervently hoping I was right about that. "And you're not likely to see the guy again, so..."

Sara seemed a little uneasy when I said this.

"Well, he did ask me if he could see me again before we left town."

"And what did you tell him?"

"I was noncommittal. I said I didn't know whether I'd have time. So he gave me his phone number just in case."

Knowing Sara, I was sure she was hoping to find a way to see this guy again. And as long as it didn't compromise our mission in some way, that was fine with me.

"So overall," I said, "it sounds like you had a good time." I hoped I didn't sound jealous.

"I sure did." She scratched her head and seemed to be concentrating.

"At least what I can remember of it."

****

The day's work turned out to be fairly brief. I had wanted to sound out some of my ideas with Sara, and once she had showered and we had had breakfast, she was willing to postpone further sightseeing and listen. It always helps to explain a plan to someone else, because in the explaining whatever flaws it has, whatever has been overlooked or conveniently shunted aside, will probably be exposed. It's the familiar "now that I say it, it doesn't sound very good" syndrome. Besides, Sara is very good at spotting those flaws and pointing them out. But after an hour of this, it occurred to me that we still were not really ready to finalize any plans.

"You know, I can't really do much more until Aaron gets back," I complained to Sara with a sigh just before noon. "We have to integrate him into the plan, get him up to speed. We have to describe what we've seen and done, what we expect him to do."

"And he may have some ideas of his own that we—or more accurately you—haven't thought of,"

Sara added.

"Yeah, that's what I'm afraid of. I'm sure he still thinks this is just a matter of waltzing into Sanders' house, picking up his violin, and waltzing out again." I shook my head. "Amateurs! Watch out for amateurs!"

"Hey, don't get ahead of yourself. Give him a chance. And don't forget you're not exactly a grizzled veteran yourself."

"Right. Okay, we'll see," I said, but rather grudgingly.

"So now that we have a little time," Sara said, "I'd sure like to do some more sightseeing in San Francisco. While we have the chance."

"I know," I said. "Me too. I do have a few things I need to do this afternoon, like check out the uniform rental shops, but that shouldn't take long."

"Great. Let's eat."

Chapter 22

Sara and I strolled down to California Street, looking for a likely place for lunch. When we passed a friendly-looking establishment called the Well Come Inn that already had a busy early lunch crowd, we joined the line inside.

The Well Come Inn was not an inn at all, but just a fancy burger bar, with a long list of "gourmet" burgers taking up most of the back wall. That was fine with us, as we didn't require anything fancy for lunch, and a burger, gourmet or pedestrian, would be quite acceptable.

We stood in line contemplating the several dozen ways the Well Come Inn could prepare a slab of chopped beef, not to mention chopped pork, chopped turkey, chopped bison, or even, for the truly adventurous, chopped wild boar and ostrich, and the equal number of buns on which it could be served: white, wheat, multi-grain, gluten-free, onion, sour dough, or naked—apparently their term for no bun at all.

"It's like getting coffee at Starbuck's, isn't it?" Sara said. "I wonder if they have a plain old cheeseburger on a soft white bun?"

"That doesn't sound very adventurous," I said.

"No, I suppose not. I guess I really should try the wild boar or the ostrich. Maybe I'll compromise and have the bison—at least it looks something like a cow."

I had to laugh, as the line edged slowly forward toward the order counter. "Since when did a buffalo look anything like a cow?"

"Hey, it looks a heck of a lot more like a cow than an ostrich or a wild boar does. Anyway, that's what I'll get. And you?"

"Hmm. Let's see. I don't see any aardvark or platypus, so maybe I'll just settle for wild boar."

"Probably tastes like chicken," Sara said.

"Probably. I'll let you know."

We ordered and received our burgers and sat down to find out whether we preferred bison and/or wild boar to beef. We didn't, but it was fun finding out.

Sara finished her bison, took a few sips of her drink, and turned to me with a serious expression. "Now that it's almost time to execute your plan," she said, "how are you feeling about the risks and rewards? Still positive?"

I thought about this for a minute or so, trying to weigh the factors on both sides. "So far as I can figure out my own motivations," I said, "I do still think it's worth the risk. There's big money involved, and a virtuoso to save from himself, not to mention myself to clear of a possible murder charge. On the other hand, there's nothing much in it for you except a paid vacation, and I wouldn't blame you if you decide you don't want any further part of my crazy adventure and head on home. I promise I wouldn't hold it against you one bit, nor would Aaron. This is our little scheme, or rather his with me as his trainer, and while you've been a huge help so far and I really appreciate it, from here on it's pretty much up to Aaron and me. So feel free to have a few more days of sightseeing on Aaron's nickel and fly home."

I wasn't just putting up a noble front. I'd felt uneasy from the beginning about getting Sara directly involved in what I knew was a risky caper, and the riskier it looked, the guiltier I felt. I would more than understand Sara bowing out after doing her part of the groundwork. In fact, my conscience would have preferred it.

Sara didn't immediately respond. It was obvious that she too was conflicted, between her loyalty to me and her sense of self-preservation. At the moment, neither side seemed to be winning.

After a minute, Sara said, "Let me sleep on that. For now, I'll just stay in the background and you do whatever it is you decide to do. I'll wait until Aaron gets back to decide whether to stick around or wait for you at home."

"Fair enough," I said. I was relieved the matter had been put over for a while. And although I still had not completely resolved the risk-benefit issue, the very fact that it remained unresolved meant I would probably go ahead with my plan, having failed sufficiently to talk myself out of it.

But I too would sleep on it.

Back at the hotel, I again looked over my plans, as Sara watched some crime show (naturally) on TV. We were both avoiding any further discussion of either my motivations or her intentions.

Then the phone rang.

Chapter 23

There is a tendency for someone with a guilty conscience, such as a lady who is planning a major heist, not to mention her unwilling accomplice, to become jumpy at a sudden summons from beyond, whether a knock on the door or the ringing of a phone. Have we somehow been found out? Has retribution come to call even before the crime was committed?

Sara and I stayed still, giving each other the same "who could that be" look, and the phone rang four times before Sara finally reached over and answered it.

"Yes?" Sara's greeting was tentative, her features wary, her eyes on me. I held my breath. I knew this feeling was uncharacteristic of me, but I couldn't seem to help it.

Suddenly, however, Sara's features relaxed and she smiled. "Oh, hi! It's great to hear from you."

I exhaled.

Sara put her hand over the mouthpiece and whispered, "It's Aaron. He's back in town!

"Let me put you on the speaker," Sara said into the phone. "If there is one…wait…okay, here it is…" Sara pressed the speaker button. "There. Okay, start again."

Over the speaker we heard, "I'm back. How are you guys?"

"Welcome home!" I said. I skipped telling how we were. I'm sure my voice reflected both relief that it was not the outside world closing in, and genuine pleasure in hearing Aaron's voice again. "Where are you?"

"I'm at the airport. Actually, the Oakland airport; it was much easier to get a flight here than to SFO. I'm on the ground and walking toward baggage claim."

"Did you just get in?"

"Yeah. I was going to surprise you guys, but then I thought since I'm only a few miles away—less than a half hour, I'm sure—it wouldn't pay to go to the hassle of renting a car and then turning it in. I was hoping you'd come and get me here. A lot more pleasant than a taxi or shuttle. I assume you still have the car you rented."

I laughed. "Well, not the same car, but we do have *a* car. I'll explain later. And yes, I'm sure we'll be glad to come and pick you up." I looked over at Sara, who nodded her approval.

"Great! I'll wait out front, Terminal 1, where the taxis and such pick people up. What kind of car are you driving?"

This was a more difficult question than Aaron realized. We had been through so many cars in the past few days, at the moment I couldn't remember exactly which one we were driving, despite having just been riding in it.

Sara came to my rescue.

"A BMW convertible," she said into the phone. "White, with red upholstery."

Of course she'd remember that. Highlight of her trip so far.

Aaron chuckled. "You girls go first class. Fine with me. I'll see you in about an hour, okay?"

"We'll be there," Sara said enthusiastically, and she hung up the phone.

I looked over at Sara, who was all smiles. "Does this mean you're still in?"

"I guess so," Sara said. "Now that Aaron's back, we're finally getting to the good part."

****

It was about forty minutes after we returned from the airport before Aaron, who had retired to his suite to freshen up, finally made an appearance. He knocked on the door of 507 and this time I was the one who opened it.

"It's that violinist again," I called back to Sara. "You know, the one they tried to foist on us when we ordered a cellist. Should I let him in?"

Sara's face became thoughtful as she considered the matter.

"I suppose so. They're probably still out of cellists."

I smiled and stepped back, bowing a bit and sweeping Aaron into the room.

Aaron settled himself on the sofa with a contented sigh.

"Want anything to drink from the minibar?" I asked. "It's expensive, but it's on the guy who's paying for this place, so don't worry about it."

Aaron laughed. "In that case, I'll have a beer. And help yourself, of course."

I did, handing bottles of beer to Aaron and Sara and taking one myself.

The formalities having been observed, I got down to business.

"Do you want to hear what we've been doing since

you left us?"

"Of course. But first I have something here for you guys." He reached into his pocket and withdrew two small packages, ivory-colored bags tied at the top with thin red cord. He handed one to each of us.

This was unexpected, and a bit exciting. "What are these?" I asked, feeling the soft texture of the bag in my hand.

"Open it and see."

Sara and I both opened our bags, and almost simultaneously drew a sharp breath on extracting the contents. Each of us was holding a delicate gold chain on which was suspended an exquisite little replica of a violin, fashioned in 24-carat gold.

"It's lovely," Sara exclaimed, her eyes wide.

"Beautiful," I added. "But why…"

"Just because," Aaron said, obviously pleased at our reaction. "A guy can't go away on a trip and not bring something back for his favorite two ladies."

"But where did you find them?" I asked. "They're perfect."

"I had a few hours between rehearsals, so I took a stroll on Wilshire Boulevard. I passed a little jewelry shop and saw these, or actually one of them, in the window. I had been meaning to find something to bring back for you, but all I'd seen was the usual souvenir crap, and I didn't have time to really go shopping. When I saw the tiny violin, I thought what a perfect way to symbolize our little enterprise; but of course I needed two of them." He looked over at Sara, who blushed a little.

"I went into the store and asked the clerk if they had a second one. He went and got the owner, who said they only had the one, but he could get another for me by the next day. So I paid for both and had him deliver them to my hotel. They arrived just before I left. Now put them on. I want you to wear them for the rest of our adventure; that is, if you like them well enough."

I looked at Sara, who was already fitting her violin around her neck, and said to Aaron, "We love them. Here, help me put mine on."

I went over to Aaron and handed him the chain ends, showed him what to press to open the clasp, and standing almost against him, turned around so he could slip the violin over my head and fasten the clasp. I admit I felt a little chill go down my spine when his hands brushed the back of my neck, which was strange because his hands were quite warm.

"But what about you?" Sara asked. "We can't have the three musketeers with only two…two…muskets."

Aaron laughed. "That occurred to me, but I can't exactly wear a necklace; or if I can I'd rather not. But that's okay, because remember I have the real violin. Or I will have it when we take it back. So it works out perfectly: You two have the models, and when we complete our mission I'll have the original and it will sort of close the circle."

I thought about that and decided I liked the symbolism.

"Works for me," I said, and I put my arms around Aaron and gave him a big thank-you kiss. Sara came over and did the same. Aaron clearly felt he had been more than rewarded for his gifts. He hadn't mentioned what they had cost him, which must have been at least a thousand dollars. He probably wondered at that moment what he might have received in gratitude if he had.

Chapter 24

Once Sara and I had tucked our new necklaces into our blouses and Aaron had resumed his seat on the sofa, we took chairs opposite him and I steered the meeting back to business.

"Okay, now shall I tell you what we've been up to?"

"Absolutely," Aaron said. "Right from the beginning to picking me up at the airport."

I described in detail everything important that had occurred, including the comings and goings of Sanders, his employees, and the cleaning crew.

Aaron asked a few questions, but mostly he just listened, nodding at the appropriate times and shaking his head in disbelief at others. When I had finished, he said, "I think we should let this rest for today, and tomorrow, when everyone's fresh, you can tell me where we go from here, kind of lay out the plan. That okay?"

Sara and I nodded. "That's fine," I said, "but we really have to get started in earnest tomorrow. We have to show up at Sanders' place next Thursday morning without fail."

"No problem," Aaron assured me. He glanced at his watch. "Meanwhile, it's almost seven. Let's go downstairs and have dinner. I'll make a reservation and pick you up in a half hour, okay?"

That sounded fine, and we readily agreed. Aaron stood up and made his way to the door. Both Sara and I met him there and gave him a group hug, so that he likely was feeling quite warm when he finally reached the hallway and headed for the elevator.

The temperature in our suite was elevated as well. As soon as the door closed behind Aaron, we both pulled out our new necklaces and admired them.

"These must have cost him a fortune," Sara remarked. I knew a thing or two about the value of jewelry, and agreed.

"What a doll," Sara continued. "I sure hope we can get him his violin back."

I agreed with that also. And I noted that Sara, who only a few hours earlier had seemed on the verge of abandoning us and going back to Seattle (which I would have considered quite justified), seemed now to be fully invested in the enterprise. Maybe she felt she couldn't abandon Aaron after taking his expensive gift. Whatever the reason, Aaron's reappearance had clearly sealed the deal.

The troops were in line and ready for battle.

****

Half an hour later, Aaron picked us up and we made our way to the Tonga Room.

"This time," I said to Sara as we waited to be seated, "we'll have Aaron to protect us if any guys try to pick us up."

"Pick you up?" Aaron said. "Where?"

"When we were here the other evening," I said.

"I see. I guess that just shows I can't leave you girls on your own. Flirting with guys in fancy restaurants…"

"We weren't flirting," I insisted. "We were just sitting and minding our own business. This is flirting." I batted my eyes theatrically and gave Aaron a "come hither" look in my best imitation of Mae West.

Aaron laughed. "I thought flirting was supposed to attract guys, not scare them off."

I gave Aaron a friendly shove. "I guess it all depends what you're attracted to," I said.

Before Aaron could tell me what he was attracted to, the maître d' came over and said our table was ready.

****

Once the three of us were seated and had ordered dinner, Sara and I insisted Aaron tell us all about his adventure in Los Angeles. He regaled us with some of the more interesting features of his engagement there, including some amusing anecdotes about backstage mishaps. He was looking around the restaurant when he suddenly became more serious.

Turning to look earnestly at Sara and me, he said, "Listen, there's something I want to tell you, something that might possibly pose a problem for our enterprise."

I sure didn't like the sound of that. "So what did you do, confess to the cops and throw yourself on the mercy of the court? Or did you discover that you had the real violin after all?"

Aaron didn't seem amused. "No, no, nothing like that. It's actually a little hard to explain."

"Well, now that you've started—"

"Yes, of course. I was going to tell you later, but it turns out this is the best time to do it. It's like this: Don't look now, but there's a young woman sitting over there next to the philodendron."

Of course, both Sara and I had to look, although we tried to be discreet about it. Sitting next to a tall green plant was a young woman sipping a dark red colored drink and looking in our general direction. She appeared to be in her very early twenties. Long blond hair framed a girlish but attractive face.

"That's a dracaena, not a philodendron," Sara said after she had turned back around.

"Are you sure it isn't a rubber plant?" I asked.

"Will you please stop debating the plant," Aaron said more loudly than he probably intended. "I'm talking about the woman, not the plant!"

"Okay, tell us about the woman," I said. "Good-looking gal; a little young for you, though."

"That's the point. Or rather, it's not exactly the point, but it's part of the point."

"You're not making any sense," I said. "First you have us look at a potted plant, then you tell us the point is the woman next to the plant, and then she's only part of the point. Maybe you should start at the beginning."

Aaron rolled his eyes upward, made what appeared to be a short silent prayer for strength, and began:

"The young woman's name is Jennifer Logan. I met her at the airport when I arrived in L.A. last week, while I was waiting for my suitcase. She was kind of wandering aimlessly around the baggage claim area looking lost, and I asked if I could help. She said her luggage hadn't arrived, and she didn't know what to do about it. It was only the second or third time she'd ever taken a plane and the first time her luggage hadn't shown up. Well, I've lost my share of luggage—that is, the airlines have lost their share of my luggage—over the years, and I know the routine pretty well."

"So you played Sir Galahad and helped her find her luggage?" Sara asked.

"You might say that. Only we didn't find the luggage, at least not right then. I showed her where to go to report the missing suitcase. A little while later she came back and said that they told her it had been located but was in some godforsaken place like Nome, Alaska, or maybe it was Timbuktu, but wherever it was, it would take until the next day to show up.

"I thought that was the end of the matter. But then she starts to cry and I ask what's wrong and she says all of her clothes and most of her money are in the suitcase and she has nowhere to stay overnight until the suitcase arrives and…well…"

"Don't tell me," I said, "that you offered to pay for her hotel room or something."

"More the 'something,' I'm afraid," Aaron said, and now he was looking decidedly sheepish. That wasn't a good sign.

"I'm almost afraid to ask," I said. But of course I had to. Or more accurately I didn't have to. Aaron hesitated a few seconds before answering.

"Well, I invited her to stay with me at my hotel overnight. Just until she could get her suitcase the next day. I had an extra day before my first rehearsal, and she seemed so…so…needy."

"I see," I said. "At least I think I see where this is leading. So did you sleep with the girl?"

"Flo," Sara interjected before Aaron could answer. "That's none of our business. If Aaron wants to—"

"I have a feeling it is our business," I said, "or Aaron wouldn't be telling us this story, and he certainly wouldn't look like he'd just eaten that cookie his mother told him to leave for after dinner."

In fact, Aaron's features had now changed from sheepish to outright guilty, with a large dose of miserable. He nevertheless soldiered on.

"Let's just say she and I shared some intimate moments and leave it at that."

"Were these 'intimate moments' in bed, by any chance?"

Sara again interrupted before Aaron could respond, assuming he was going to respond. "Flo! What difference does it make?"

"Look," Aaron said, "it was late, we were both tired, she was scared. I was just comforting her. If you must know, we didn't...do what you're thinking. We were in bed together, yes, but I was so tired from the long day and the flight, I just fell asleep before it became an issue. In fact, she probably thought I was gay or something, because I didn't try anything."

At this I'm afraid I rolled my eyes. "But you would have if you hadn't been so tired," I said, and Sara kicked me under the table. Maybe justifiably.

"The point is," Aaron continued, ignoring the question, "that what I considered a passing moment and a good deed she apparently considered more...more meaningful. The next morning they delivered her suitcase, we parted, and I assumed that would be the last I'd see of her."

"So the fact that she's over there by the potted palm, or whatever the hell it is, isn't just an odd coincidence?" Sara said.

"I'm afraid not. She showed up in the audience at each of my performances in L.A. and each time tried to get backstage to see me after the recital. I refused to see her, figuring she'd get discouraged."

"Apparently not," I said, taking another furtive glance at Ms. Logan.

"No. And now here she is. I don't know how she knew where I was going, or how she managed to get here herself so quickly, but, well, here she is."

"So what you're telling us is that you're being stalked by a lovesick and very determined would-be groupie."

"Yes, I guess that sorta sums it up. I'm not concerned about the fact that she's following me. I mean, it could be a nuisance at some point, but I figure if I keep avoiding her, she'll eventually give up—or run out of money to fly everywhere I do."

"Unless she gets violent," I offered.

"She really doesn't strike me as the violent type."

"Hmmm" was all that I responded. Looks could be deceiving, although I had to admit she did look like she would make an unlikely serial killer.

"Anyway, what I'm concerned about is that if we're going to be engaging in…in questionable activities, as we've discussed, the last thing we need is someone watching over our shoulder, or even at a distance."

I looked at Sara, and for a moment neither of us said anything. I just raised my eyebrows. Then Sara said, "I see what you mean. I'd be nervous enough just going through with the plan. I certainly wouldn't want to be doing it under observation."

As for me, I was already deep in thought. I quickly came to a decision. "No, you're right," I said to Aaron. "We have to find a way to discourage your little friend without arousing her suspicion that there's something we don't want her to know."

"Any ideas how we can do that?" Aaron asked.

"I'm thinking. I'm thinking." I sat and thought while Aaron and Sara looked at me and tried to avoid looking in the direction of Jennifer Logan, who had by this time finished her dark red drink and was starting on what appeared to be a latte.

It was at least five minutes of strained silence before I finally said, to no one in particular, "What we have to do is discourage her from following Aaron. That means either grab her and stuff her in a suitcase, or threaten her with grave bodily harm if she doesn't take the next flight home, or somehow change her mind about wanting to follow—or talk to, or sleep with—Aaron." I looked at the other two and concluded, "I take it we'd rather keep things nonviolent, which means making Aaron less desirable in her eyes. Correct?"

Aaron and Sara nodded in agreement.

"Okay, then, there are a few ways we can make Aaron seem less attractive to her. One, we could change his appearance from being the irresistible hunk he is to something more ordinary, more mundane." I indicated this choice by raising my index finger. But I'm sure they could tell from the way I said it that this was not meant as a serious suggestion.

"No," Sara said with a straight face, "it'd be like defacing the Mona Lisa. Unthinkable."

"Very funny," Aaron said.

Good line. I smiled and continued, raising a second finger, "Two, Aaron could confront her and tell her to get lost, maybe insult her a bit and send her away crying. She'd go home and find another celebrity to bother."

Aaron was shaking his head before I finished.

"I'm sorry, but I just can't do that. She's really a very nice girl, and I couldn't treat her that way. I don't think I could treat anyone that way, but especially someone like Jennifer. I mean, it's not her fault we're planning something illegal—"

"Shhh!" I said and covered Aaron's mouth. I looked around to see if anyone seemed to be listening. No one was. "Okay, we get the point." I raised a third finger. "Third, we can convince her of some other feature of his personality that will discourage her, or at least lessen her attraction to him."

"And did you have any particular feature in mind?" Aaron asked. "Perhaps tell her I'm a fugitive from justice? Or a vegetarian? Or I don't change my socks regularly?"

"You don't? Now you tell me," I said. "No, I had something else in mind. Something you said about what happened in your hotel room gave me an idea."

"What was that? All I said was that we kind of got cozy in bed and I fell asleep."

"You were too tired to have sex with her?"

"That's right. No, I mean, even if I'd wanted to have sex with her, which I didn't say I did. Want to, that is." Aaron seemed to be tripping over his hasty clarifications.

"Yes, yes, I understand," I said. "But then the question is, do you think she wanted to have sex with you?"

"How should I know?" Aaron's innocent tone was almost convincing.

Sara and I exchanged "Oh, sure" looks. I shook my head and said, "You mean you can't tell if a sweet young thing in bed next to you is coming on to you? Really?"

Aaron looked down at the table before answering. "Well, okay. I guess if you put it that way, she was kind of snuggling up and making like she wanted to…to pursue matters further. But I was too tired." Then he quickly added, "And not interested anyway."

I ignored the qualification. "That's what I thought. And I'll bet that if our Ms. Logan thought that there was no chance of having sex with Aaron in the future, that the best she might accomplish is some conversation about violin history and a few warm hugs, she wouldn't think it worth the time, effort, and cost of following him from place to place."

"What makes you think so?"

"Well, think about it," I said. "People only stalk other people for certain reasons. The paparazzi do it to get pictures, reporters to get a story, process servers to serve papers, and so forth. But when it's infatuation that motivates a nubile young woman with raging hormones, you can bet it isn't pictures or stories they're after. Or warm hugs, for that matter. I've read about the groupies who follow rock stars around—not to mention tennis and golf stars and other celebrities—and it ain't just for autographs, I can assure you. So I repeat, if Ms. Logan thought there was nothing but a strictly platonic relationship awaiting her if she caught up with Aaron, I think chances are good she'd give it up as a lost cause."

There was a short silence as Aaron and Sara digested this proposition. Then Sara said, "I'm not sure I agree, but I don't have any better idea. So assuming you're right, how do we convince the young lady that there's no sex at the end of the rainbow?"

Aaron jumped in: "And castration is strictly out!"

Sara and I turned and stared at him, and Sara began to laugh. I leaned over and put my arm around Aaron and assured him that nothing so drastic would be necessary. I then went on to explain my idea, Aaron and Sara listening intently. Aaron contributed an occasional "Absolutely not!" or "You must be joking," but I managed to soothe his feelings and dampen his objections. When I had finished, Aaron said, with more resignation than enthusiasm, "Okay, I guess it's worth a try."

The script had passed its first big test.

Chapter 25

We three conspirators were assembled in Aaron's suite on Sunday morning, a council of war. We had put off dealing with Jennifer Logan until we had taken care of what we considered more important business. It was time to make final preparations for the campaign. Aaron had ordered snacks and drinks from room service. An army councils best on a full stomach.

Sara and I went back over some of the salient details of our reconnaissance in Los Altos.

When we had finished discussing the facts on the ground, I described the outlines of my plan.

"I think the easiest way to get into the house is as part of the cleaning crew. They come on Thursdays, so next Thursday is when we would plan to pull this off."

"With you posing as a maid?" Aaron asked.

"Sure. That's one line of work I'm thoroughly familiar with, so I can bring it off pretty easily."

"You mean like your maid act in my hotel in Seattle?" Aaron said, a twinkle in his eye.

"Yes, like that. I had no problems passing for a housekeeper there."

"Or for a burglar," he teased.

Sara jumped in. "Cut it out, will you? We'll take it as given that in Seattle, Flo made a better maid than a burglar. We assume this time will be different."

Aaron raised his hands in surrender. "Sorry. Go on,

please."

"Thank you. Now as I say, I should have no trouble passing as a maid. It's you who might have a problem."

"Me? What do you mean me? How the hell can I pass as a maid?"

I smiled. "If not as a maid, just how did you plan to get into Sanders' house?"

Aaron scratched his head. He took a few peanuts from a dish on the coffee table and chewed thoughtfully on them. "I hadn't really thought about it. I don't know, as a…a plumber? A carpet cleaner? An exterminator?"

"And what if they don't happen to need a plumber next Thursday, and their carpets are clean and they don't have a bug problem? How will you get in then?"

"Yeah, I see that, but a maid? C'mon."

"It isn't all that difficult. We get you a wig and some stage makeup, you wear pants to cover your hairy legs—at least I assume they're hairy—and a scarf that covers as much of the top of you as possible."

Aaron sat there trying to picture himself in the disguise I had just described. He shook his head slowly.

"I don't know. I'm sure you can pass as a maid, but I don't think I'll fool anyone, wig or no wig."

I was exasperated. "I agree, and that's exactly what I've been trying to tell you from the first time you asked me to help get your violin back. If you just let me do it by myself, we have a much better chance of success than if you continue to insist on coming along." I had been hoping that Aaron would eventually see my point and agree I should carry on alone.

Unfortunately, Aaron saw it differently. Shaking his head slowly, he said, "I'm sorry, but I'm still coming along. I mean, you're right. I'm making it harder for you to do your job and more likely that we'll get caught. But I still want to do this myself. That is, with your help. I'll understand if you decide at this late stage not to do it at all, because it's too risky with me along. Then I'll just try it myself, even if I have to dress up like a girl to do it. Hell, I might be pretty attractive as a cross-dresser!"

I saw it was useless to argue, and I really didn't want to reopen the debate over Aaron's participation. He obviously had an obsession about getting his prize possession back himself, and because it was clearly more emotional than rational, I was not likely to talk him out of it. And I certainly was not going to let him go out there himself; it would be like sending a lamb into a wolf pack.

"Okay," I said, "let's get back to the plan. We go in posing as cleaners on Thursday."

Aaron leaned over and kissed me on the cheek. "Hmph," was my only response, but I guess I did smile a bit.

Sara saw she had better get us back on track.

"How do you fool the real maids, or the Sanders people if they know the real maids?" she asked me.

"Good question," Aaron added.

"Yes, it is a good question. Here's what I plan to do: On Thursday morning I'll call the TidyHome Maid Service and tell them I'm calling for Sanders and because he has some important meeting at the house that day, they should skip this week's service. Of course I'll generously offer on his behalf to pay for the week's service anyway." I took a sip of coffee to give them time to consider this and continued, "Then I'll call the Sanders house and tell them I'm from the maid service and their regular crew had to be diverted for an emergency of some kind and they're sending a substitute crew."

Aaron considered this. "I like that idea. But since you're telling them it's a new crew anyway, why not just say it'll be a couple, a man and a woman? Maybe he's one of the supervisors or something and they're short-handed because of the emergency. That way we don't risk them seeing through some silly disguise or noticing I have a pretty low voice and large biceps for a woman."

It was my turn to consider. Maybe Aaron had a point there. Maybe I was being stubborn about his being along and was just trying to make it harder for him, at the same time making it harder for myself as well.

"I hate to admit it," I said, "but you might be right. I've never encountered a male housecleaner myself, but I do know there are a few out there, like male secretaries or receptionists or…"

"Or ballet dancers?" Sara put in.

"Thank you. That's very helpful." To Aaron: "Actually, men often do the really tough house cleaning, the kind you need after a fire or flood. We can say you're experienced in our disaster cleanup service or something and just helping out."

"What if they don't have a disaster cleanup service?" Sara asked.

"They do now."

Aaron looked much relieved. "Good. Then that's settled. We replace the maid service. That gives us pretty much the run of the house, doesn't it?"

"Well, maybe, depending whether certain areas are

off limits to the cleaners. But we'll have to cross that bridge later. Meanwhile, I have to locate the uniform company that supplies TidyHome and rent a uniform that looks like theirs."

"What about my uniform?" Aaron asked.

I thought about this. "Good question. I doubt they'll have men's uniforms, though I can ask. If not, we'll buy you a shirt and pants that matches the colors of the maid's uniform. That should be close enough. I hardly think they'd expect a male cleaner to wear an aproned skirt and blouse."

"God, I hope not!" said Aaron with feeling.

"I also have to get a few other important items, like a special carrier built for cleaning supplies."

"Yeah, I guess the police probably confiscated your burglar tools," Sara said, with just a hint of a smirk. I ignored it. "What kind of special carrier?" she asked.

"Something that will have big brushes and such on top, and a false bottom that'll hold a Guarneri violin."

Aaron nodded. "Which means you'll need the dimensions of the violin, right?"

"Right. And I'll need several hundred dollars to get someone to build it in a day or two."

"No doubt. Anything else?"

"Just a few odds and ends. And of course you'll also have to wear a disguise of some kind."

"Why? We just decided I could go as a man."

"Yes, but not as Aaron Levy, the well-known celebrity. What if someone at the house is a music lover and just happens to know what you look like? One of them actually got close enough to steal your violin, remember? Hell, they might even be big fans of yours.

Like Jennifer." I really didn't have to add that last part, but I couldn't resist. "They did covet your violin, so they definitely know who you are."

"Okay, point taken. I'll get some kind of moustache or beard or something. Okay?"

I laughed. "Yes, that should do fine."

"Is there anything I can do to help?" Sara asked. "Would you like me to put on a moustache or a wig too? I hate to be left out."

"Oh, I think you're just fine being left out," I said. "In fact, let's hope you stay that way. If we need you for backup, it won't be because everything went according to plan."

"So what do we do now?" Aaron asked. "Synchronize our watches?"

Sara had the answer to that. "No, we go downstairs and eat. I understand they have a fabulous Sunday brunch buffet."

Hearing no objection to her part of the plan, Sara rose and headed for the door, grabbing her purse on the way. Aaron winked at me, rose and offered his arm, and thus we followed Sara to the elevator.

Some plans require no discussion at all.

Chapter 26

Sunday afternoon, and it was time to deal with Jennifer. According to our plan, at 4:00, after an ostentatious saunter through the lobby (where he had noticed his young stalker sitting), Aaron entered the hotel café, which advertised a British-style afternoon tea. Few tables were yet taken, and Aaron sat down at a table easily observable from almost every other part of the room. Immediately a waiter came over to take his order. A few minutes later, he had before him a bone china cup and saucer and a steaming pot of tea. Not long afterward, Ms. Jennifer Logan entered the café. After glancing around the room and noticing Aaron sitting by himself, she chose a table about twenty feet away. Like Aaron, she was served almost as soon as she sat down.

My plan had assumed that Jennifer would take her time assessing the situation before making some kind of attempt to join Aaron at his table. Sara and I were to use some pretext to sit down at her table first and start a conversation with her. Unfortunately, Jennifer immediately threw the plan into disarray. As soon as she had poured her tea, she got up, teacup in hand, and headed straight for Aaron's table. Clearly she was going to make a frontal assault without wasting time with reconnaissance or strategic maneuvers. Obviously an amateur.

Sara and I, who had been watching from the side of the room since Aaron first entered, knew we had to act quickly. I grabbed an empty teacup that had been abandoned nearby, turned to Sara, and said, "Follow me." Calculating the trajectory and velocity needed to intercept Jennifer on her way to her intended target, I began walking quickly in the young woman's direction, Sara close behind. When I was about two feet away, I turned as if to say something to Sara and "accidentally" collided with the startled Jennifer, spilling her cup of tea onto her dress and the floor in about equal parts.

I was, of course, visibly appalled at my clumsiness and abjectly apologetic over the damage I had caused. Sara, taking her cue from me, commiserated with the offended woman and berated me for not watching where I was going. Jennifer tried to brush off both the spilled tea and the two pesky ladies surrounding her, but we would not be easily mollified. We offered to take the victim over to our table (any table that was vacant and we could claim as ours) and replace the tea we had spilled.

"That's really not necessary," Jennifer insisted, as she dabbed at the wet patch on her dress with a hanky and tried to regain her composure. "I'm fine. No harm done. Really." She smiled weakly to emphasize her point.

But Sara and I were adamant. "I'd never forgive myself," I said, "if I didn't at least buy you another pot of tea and help you dry off." And before Jennifer could protest any further, Sara and I, practically carrying Jennifer between us, maneuvered her to the nearest empty table, sat her down, and called over a waiter.

"What kind of tea did I spill on you?" I asked.

Jennifer was still flustered, but she answered weakly, "It was mint, I think. But you really—"

"Nonsense," I responded and gave the order to the waiter, together with mine and Sara's. Then I dabbed at Jennifer's wet dress with a cloth napkin and assumed what I hoped was a caring, sisterly manner and tone.

"My name is Florence—you can call me Flo—and this is Sara."

Apparently resigning herself to this accidental tea party, Jennifer said, "I'm Jennifer. Jennifer Logan."

We exchanged polite conversation about the weather and the benefits of herbal tea for a few minutes as Jennifer became more comfortable with her unexpected new friends. I then brought the conversation around to where I had intended.

"You seemed to be headed in the direction of Aaron Levy's table. Do you know him?"

Jennifer hesitated a moment before answering, "Uh…sort of. I met him last week in Los Angeles."

"Really. You know, Sara and I spent quite a while talking with him yesterday."

Jennifer looked more closely at her two companions. "I thought I recognized you. I saw you at his table." It was, of course, the presence of us two women at Aaron's table that had kept her from approaching him on that earlier occasion.

"Yes," I admitted, "Mr. Levy is Sara's and my absolute favorite violinist. We go to every concert of his we can and have all of his recordings. And when we saw him by himself we just couldn't resist asking if we could join him."

Jennifer accepted this information neutrally, perhaps not certain whether these older ladies were to be admired as fellow groupies or resented as rivals for Aaron's attention. "Oh, I see," was all she responded.

I continued, finally getting to the most important part of our charade: "Yes, and you won't believe some of the things we found out about Mr. Levy once he'd had a few drinks and we'd all become, well, friends."

"Uh, good things?" Jennifer asked.

"Oh, neither good nor bad, right Sara?"

Sara, finally getting a chance to enter the conversation, said, "Right. Just interesting things you would never guess about someone so famous. I mean usually there's nothing about these public personalities that hasn't been discovered and written about a hundred times over."

I could see that Jennifer's curiosity was quickly growing, to the point that now if we had told her tea was over and she could continue on her way to Aaron's table, she probably would have refused to leave until she had all the details of what these weird ladies had learned.

But of course no such refusal was to be necessary. Sara and I were only too glad to pass along the extraordinary information we had acquired.

"Well," I began, lowering my voice and adopting a conspiratorial tone, "Sara and I were not only anxious to meet our favorite violinist, but I'll admit we were hoping we might, shall we say, spend some quality time with him." I didn't exactly wink at Jennifer, but I did try to assume that "you know what I mean" look on my face. I checked to see that the young woman had taken the hint. From the latter's expression, she had.

"When we got around to suggesting the three of us might meet for drinks and a little socializing after dinner, Mr. Levy seemed very uneasy," I continued. "When we pressed the issue a bit more, he finally came out and told us why he'd rather not accept our offer."

"And why was that?" Jenner asked. "Don't tell me he's married and his wife and kids are staying with him. I thought he was a bachelor." She looked genuinely alarmed, either at the prospect of Aaron's marriage or at her having failed to notice something so obvious.

I was suddenly sorry I hadn't thought of that particular ploy, which sounded even better than the one I was working on; but it was too late for that now.

"No, nothing like that," I assured her. "But just as much of a problem, maybe more."

Jennifer was getting impatient. "So what was the problem? Something about you and Sara?"

"You might say that. More something about all of us ladies." I looked around and lowered my voice.

"He's gay."

****

Several seconds went by in silence. I looked at Jennifer and tried to read her expression. I had a sudden vision of Jennifer deciding it was her duty to change Aaron's mind about women, to show him what he was missing. Doubtless more than one woman, especially unsophisticated and infatuated women, have made such an effort, as if sexual preference, like electrical current, could be changed from AC to DC, so to speak, with the flick of a switch. I was preparing to talk her out of such a plan while Jennifer, realizing her mouth was hanging open, closed it. The young woman began to say something like "Don't give me that shit," but stopped herself. She was considering it. And gradually her face was turning a soft shade of red.

"You know," she said after a minute or two, "come to think of it, that would explain why he…what happened when we…when I met him in L.A."

Sara and I were both tempted to ask Jennifer what happened in L.A., but we both already knew, and it was obvious Jennifer would rather not elaborate to near-strangers on her abortive roll in the hay with Aaron.

Jennifer asked, "Did he come right out and say that? That he's gay?"

I had not actually come up with the details of our supposed conversation with Aaron, so I was momentarily at a loss to answer. Sara saved the day by jumping in with, "Oh, he didn't come right out and say, 'Sorry girls, but I prefer boys' or anything like that. He was very nice about it and said something like, 'I'd love to, ladies, but the fellow I live with might not understand.' Kept it cool."

Jennifer seemed satisfied with Sara's answer, and I breathed a quiet sigh of relief.

Just then, as we all looked toward Aaron's table, Jennifer with new eyes, a good-looking young man of about twenty-five, with a well-toned, well-tanned physique, strode up to Aaron, said a few words, then sat down next to him. They conversed amiably for a while, and Aaron got out his wallet and put some money on the table to pay his check. The two men then stood up and, with the newcomer leading the way, left the café.

We three ladies looked at one another. My arched eyebrows communicated my thoughts. Sara commented, "Oh well, it's always that way, isn't it," leaving Jennifer to interpret the way to which Sara was referring. As for Jennifer, she clearly had seen enough. She looked at her watch, smiled at Sara and me, and said, "You'll have to excuse me. I need to change my plane reservation and I'll just have time."

I was all innocence, of course. "Oh? I was hoping the three of us could get together tomorrow, maybe for lunch. When will you be leaving?"

"Tomorrow, if I can get a reservation. I had planned to stay a bit longer, but…but I've remembered something I need to do at home and I think it would be best if I left as soon as I can."

Sara and I exchanged a look that might be interpreted as "Yes!" with a fist pump, but more discreet. Sara said to Jennifer, "What a shame, and with us just getting to know each other. But if you have to go, you have to go. Maybe we'll meet again sometime." Jennifer probably hoped not.

And with that and a few more parting pleasantries, Jennifer was gone.

I exhaled loudly. "You know, for a minute there I was afraid my plan was going to backfire and that little idiot was going to stick around and try to 'reform' Aaron."

"C'mon, do you think that's possible?"

"No, but I was still afraid she'd try. Anyway, it looks like we dodged that bullet and she's going home."

"Yeah, and I think what did it was him going off with that young hunk. What luck that guy showed up when he did; must be someone Aaron knows from somewhere."

I had to laugh. "That wasn't luck, and Aaron had never met him before now. I found him at a sports equipment store we passed. And remind me to drop by later and give him fifty dollars. Not bad pay for five minutes' work, don't you think?"

Chapter 27

Monday through Wednesday were spent in carrying out the various preparations we had decided upon. I found the uniform shop that serviced TidyHome—only the fourth one I called—and reserved the necessary attire. I said I was going to be doing some fill-in work for TidyHome and needed to rent a uniform like theirs. I was asked for which client I would be working. I wasn't sure why they needed to know, but reluctantly I said the Sanders home. That seemed to cause no difficulty, and when I stopped by on Tuesday the uniform was ready for me. I tried it on in the little dressing room provided for customers, looking at myself in the full-length mirror on the wall. Then I saw why they needed to know: Sanders required special arrangements. The uniform, what there was of it, covered barely enough to be legal, with a deeply plunging neckline and an outrageously short skirt. It made the plain-Jane livery I wore in the Hotel Royale seem like a Girl Scout uniform in comparison.

To be frank, I looked like I'd just stepped out of one of those French farces, where the scantily-clad chambermaid gets chased from bedroom to bedroom, being pinched regularly in the derriere by the lecherous husband. Once again it was fortunate I still had the figure to more or less do it justice.

For Aaron they had an appropriate-looking

selection of coveralls, so that problem was solved.

Back at the hotel, I tried on the uniform for Sara's benefit.

Sara looked thoughtful. "Hmm, I guess I'm not surprised at the uniform, the way Aaron described Sanders," she remarked. "He probably interviewed maid services until he found one that was willing to dress with the right amount of skin showing."

"Yeah, and I can imagine the view he gets when they bend over to dust under the furniture," I said. "But then, in our case, maybe distraction is good."

It was a little trickier to find a woodworking studio that could design and build the special carrying case I wanted, and within two days. I finally found one, and they wanted a higher price for expedited service, of course, as I had expected. Hey, not my money. I was to pick it up on Wednesday morning.

Aaron and I then visited a costume shop not far from Nob Hill.

"We're going to a costume party," Aaron told the proprietor. "I'll need a false moustache and maybe a small beard."

"Will your wife also want a costume? We have a special on a Cinderella ball gown."

"No, I don't think so, thanks." Turning to me, "Right?"

"Uh, right." I was a bit distracted.

The explanation of how to apply the false moustache and beard didn't take long. Within thirty minutes we had what we needed and departed.

What I'd been distracted by was Aaron's failure to correct the impression that we were married, but of course it wouldn't have done to mention it in front of the proprietor, so I let it pass. I'm not sure why it bothered me, but it did, and afterwards I did bring the matter to his attention.

"I don't know," he responded when I quizzed him on his reason for agreeing to the sudden betrothal. "It just seemed like the easiest thing to do."

"Hmm. Okay, as long as you're careful to whom you do it." And we left it at that.

****

On Wednesday morning I picked up the supplies-cum-violin carrier, as well as a magnetic "TidyHome" sign I had ordered, having remembered the approximate design of the one on the car we saw drive up with the cleaning crew. In the afternoon Aaron and I packed a few necessities, our disguise materials, and Aaron's replica Guarneri, into still another car, this time a very plain white Chevrolet Malibu. The BMW was far too ostentatious and ritzy for a cleaning service, and besides, it had already been around the Sanders house and might be remembered.

We didn't return the BMW, however. Sara asked if she could drive it while we were away, so she could explore out of town a bit. That seemed only fair to me, and Aaron didn't mind. (The BMW was rented in my name, the Chevy in Aaron's.)

Once packed and ready, Aaron and I settled ourselves in the Chevy and headed for Los Altos. Sara saw us off. Finally just a tourist, she was staying behind at the Fairmont.

"I'm really not far away if you need me," she told me. "And I sure hope you don't need me."

I hoped so too. Fervently. I would have preferred that Sara be closer at hand, just in case, but once again I recognized that I had promised to leave Sara out of the actual burglary, and I didn't feel right insisting she be at or near the scene. Besides, if this plan went awry, I wasn't really sure what Sara could do to save it.

Probably nothing except bail us out of jail.

Chapter 28

Whistling to himself while driving, Aaron seemed to be in a good mood, neither nervous nor worried. I remarked on this, and Aaron told me, "Heck, this is the best adventure I can ever remember having. You know, I've led a pretty sheltered life. I was one of those child prodigies on the violin, and since I was about six or seven my whole life has revolved around concerts and recitals and interviews and practicing and…well, you get the idea."

"Still sounds like a pretty good life to me," I said. "I mean, you've been well compensated, wined and dined and made a fuss over. What's not to like?"

"Oh, I'm not complaining. Not at all. While it's not all glamour and champagne—it's really a helluva lot of work, day in and day out—I still enjoy playing, and the lifestyle. It's just that there isn't much time for some of the other things that make life exciting."

"Like what?"

"Well…" Aaron hesitated, choosing his words. "Well, like the opposite sex, for one thing."

I laughed. "Don't tell me you can't get a date. Rich, famous, reasonably good-looking…"

Aaron looked over at me with a hurt expression. "Only reasonably?"

"Never mind that. I'm right about the women, aren't I?"

"Well, yes and no. Yes, I don't have any shortage of opportunities to take a woman out, or I suppose to spend the night with her, if I wanted."

"What do you mean, 'if'?"

"Never mind that too. The point is that there's really no chance to build any kind of relationship, to really get to know someone, when you're constantly on the move and in the public eye. At least that's what I've found. In fact, you're the first woman—you and Sara, I mean—that I've spent more than a day or two with since…well, since my mother, I guess."

I thought about that for a moment. "I guess I should be flattered, except this is more business than pleasure."

Aaron did not respond immediately, then said, "Well, I'm having fun, anyway."

I guess that beat being miserable or nervous, and that was a good thing. After a minute I continued: "Okay, being a famous violinist cramps your style when it comes to romance. Any other downside?"

"Well, I don't have much time for myself, when I'm not performing or traveling."

"Don't you take vacations? Go skiing, that sort of thing?"

"Sure, though not very often. But that's pretty tame compared to, well, to this kind of adventure. And besides, I don't particularly like skiing. I always have to be thinking that I can't afford to break something that will affect my playing."

"You do realize," I said, "that this so-called 'adventure' could result in your breaking a lot more than an arm or leg. We could end up dead, or at least in jail."

Aaron grinned. "Yeah, exciting, isn't it?"

I gave up.

****

We checked into a small hotel, the Terrace Inn, on the outskirts of Los Altos that I had noticed when Sara and I were on our reconnaissance mission. Aaron signed us in as "Mr. and Mrs. Aaron Levy." I was pretty sure that this time the instant betrothal was to avoid appearing to be, well, unmarried. I actually appreciated that he was a bit old-fashioned that way.

We unloaded our overnight bags and "special equipment" from the car, and Aaron then suggested we go into town to find a place for dinner.

"Uh-uh, no can do," I said. "We don't want to take any chances on one of the Sanders bunch spotting us before tomorrow. We'll order in, and then we'll take a drive so I can show you the layout around Sanders' house before it gets dark."

Aaron looked disappointed, but he just said, "Okay. You want me to order? I guess there's a pizza place in town."

"Sure, thanks. I like pepperoni and mushrooms, but anything you order is fine."

"No, that sounds good." He looked up pizza delivery in the phone book he found in a nightstand drawer, then picked up the phone and dialed. Soon he had placed our order and we were watching television, waiting for the pizza to arrive.

Once dinner had been delivered and enjoyed—it turned out Los Altos, like many upscale communities, had upscale "gourmet" pizza parlors—we got back into the car and headed for La Paloma Road.

I drove, and I took Aaron around to the various

vantage points that Sara and I had found, showed him the driveway and explained the difficulty of access. By the time it began to get dark, Aaron felt that he knew the lay of the land. It made the rest of the plan easier for him to understand, as it now could be placed in a real setting, and not just in the abstract.

We returned to the Terrace Inn about eight p.m. Both of us were tired and Aaron, despite his earlier bravado, was now feeling a little nervous. He seldom suffered stage fright when he was performing, he told me, but this next performance was going to be a lot more daunting, with much higher stakes, than any previous one.

"I guess it's only natural to be a bit uneasy," he said. "But I bet you're cool as a cucumber, having been through this many times in your, uh, job."

"Actually," I said, "I'm probably just as nervous as you are, only I may not show it. I know only too well that totally unexpected things can happen on my job, especially when you don't have all the information you'd like about the place you're going to be doing it. Been there; had that happen."

"Meaning…?"

"Meaning I've had my share of little, and not so little surprises. Not so little and not so pleasant."

"Oh? Care to elaborate?"

I figured it just might make Aaron feel better if he knew even a so-called "professional" faces the unexpected, and we just have to deal with it when and if it happens.

"Okay, a little bedtime story from Auntie Flo. Once upon a time—actually about six months ago— Sara and I were sitting in a little café in Seattle when we overheard the women at the next table discussing a friend of theirs, the next-door neighbor of the older one of them, who had gone away for the weekend leaving what they referred to as 'her precious jewels' in her house. Not only that, but the house's alarm system was on the fritz. These ladies were tsk-tsking about how careless this was, saying their friend, whose name I believe was Marge, was foolish to leave her precious jewels in the empty house like that. I, on the other hand, thought it was just peachy. Here I was being handed a simple, no-risk jewel heist in an empty house with no alarm system."

"It sure sounds like an easy job," Aaron said. "If you're so inclined that way, of course."

"Of course. And yes, I was so inclined. When the ladies left, I told Sara I wanted to follow them, to see where they lived. Sara caught on right away—she knows me pretty well by now—and said she didn't want anything to do with it. Fair enough, so she went home and I followed the ladies."

"And did you find out where they lived?"

"Oh, yes, that was easy. And there was only one house next to the older lady's, so I had my target. All I had to do the next day was to wait for dark, pick the lock on the back door, and help myself. Couldn't be simpler."

"Hmm. But you said this was an example of unexpected problems, so I assume it didn't turn out to be quite that simple."

"Not quite. In fact, not even a little bit. Oh, I got into the house all right, and it was deserted and alarmless, like the women said."

"But no jewels?"

"Well, yes and no. I found jewels. It just wasn't the kind of jewels I expected."

"I don't understand. What kind was it?"

"The four-legged kind. Turns out 'precious jewels' was Marge's vicious little dog, 'Jules.' You know, J-U-L-E-S. Said so right on his collar. And as soon as I got into the house, the little bastard attacked me like I was a piece of raw steak."

Aaron laughed, which I guess was good for his mental state, if not for his opinion of his mentor.

"That's great," he said. "I'll bet you were surprised. And did you escape unscathed?"

"Well, sort of. Actually, little yappy dogs terrify me—don't ask, it goes back to my childhood—and I ended up standing on the kitchen table, just out of reach of those snapping jaws and sharp teeth. And what a racket!"

More laughter. I was beginning to think telling Aaron this story wasn't such a good idea.

"Since I don't see any ugly scars on your ankles, I assume you somehow escaped? What happened? Did the monster finally get tired of trying to kill you?"

"Are you kidding? I might've been there all night, until Marge got home and found me, or what was left of me. No, I had my phone with me and called Sara for help; told her to come running and bring a hunk of meat with her."

"She must have thought that a bit strange."

"I guess, but she's almost used to rescuing me from odd predicaments. Like the time I was hiding from a couple of killers in an outdoor privy…but that's a whole other story."

"And did she arrive with the meat?"

"Oh, yes. Turns out she'd been having a burger in some restaurant with a guy she'd just met there, in the service line—she picks 'em up wherever she goes—and when she got my panicky call, she wrapped up what was left of her sandwich, grabbed what was left of his, and ran out of the burger joint, promising to come back and buy him another one."

Aaron laughed. "Wish I'd been there to see it. So what happened then?"

"Well, luckily I'd left the back door unlocked. When Sara arrived in the kitchen I shouted she should throw the meat to the far corner of the room. As soon as she did, Jules decided a burger in the corner was better than an ankle on the table and made for the corner. I jumped down and made for the door, grabbing Sara as I went by."

"While the little carnivore was devouring the burgers?"

"While he was doing to them what he had tried to do to my ankles, yes."

Aaron was silent for a few seconds, just smiling and shaking his head slowly back and forth. Then he said, "And I take it the moral of this story is…"

"…Is get all the information you can before you begin, don't begin if you don't have enough information, and never assume you have all the information."

"Lesson learned," Aaron said. Then he looked down and said, "And by the way, with nice ankles like yours, I really can't blame little Jules for going after them."

Never having been complimented on my ankles before, and not sure whether Aaron was serious, I didn't reply.

But I smiled, and I probably blushed. Right down to my ankles.

****

After I finished my cautionary tale, we sat on the room's two uncomfortable armchairs and watched TV for a while. Then a little after nine p.m., I stood up and said, "I think we'd better turn in. We have to be up very early to get ready. I have to make those calls to the maid service and Sanders, and we have to put on your little disguise and be at the Sanders house by just after eight in the morning."

Aaron nodded and stood up too. He seemed to be looking a bit wistfully at the king-size bed (it was all they had available), but he said nothing and began taking his toiletries and pajamas out of his overnight case. I did the same, thinking I was glad Aaron didn't sleep in the buff, as that could have created a little embarrassment on someone's part, though I wasn't sure on whose. I myself often slept in a filmy nightie, but for this occasion I had brought along a more substantial flannel nightgown.

Aaron must have been thinking similar thoughts. "Ever see 'It Happened One Night'?" he asked.

"Isn't that the old Clark Gable movie where two strangers end up having to spend the night together in a motel room?"

"Yeah, that's the one. I hope you won't mind that we don't hang a blanket between us, like they did. Seems like an unnecessary precaution, doesn't it?"

"Hmm. I guess so, if you promise to behave."

"Scout's honor," Aaron said, holding up two fingers in a solemn gesture. I had a feeling he had never been a Boy Scout, but I let it pass.

I washed in the small bathroom as Aaron got undressed in the bedroom, and then we changed places. When we were both ready for bed, Aaron held the covers open for me, then tucked me in and gave me a light kiss on the forehead.

"Goodnight, Mrs. Levy," he said with a smile. "Sleep well."

I didn't mind. As I turned out the lights, I thought that it wouldn't be so bad to be snuggling under the covers with the warm male body of a temporary husband; but I quickly dismissed the thought as both unprofessional and likely fatal to the success of our plan.

There would be plenty of distractions to sort out the next morning, without adding that most distracting element of all: sex.

****

The alarm clock was set for six, plenty of time to get up and do what had to be done before setting out for Chez Sanders.

Okay, that was how it was supposed to happen. In fact, neither of us slept well, and about five a.m. we both found ourselves awake and unlikely to get back to sleep before six. I was just lying there thinking through our plans for the umpteenth time, when I felt a warm hand on my thigh. I reached down and found that my flannel nightie seemed to have ridden up as I tossed and turned during the night, and now it covered only the top half or so of my body. Taking advantage of this opening, Aaron had placed his hand where the nightie had been. He was obviously waiting to see whether I would quietly remove it, roughly remove it, or scream bloody murder.

This called for some very quick calculations. On the one hand, as I had already observed, sex was probably the most distracting detour we could make on this journey. On the other hand, we had the time, Aaron apparently had the inclination, and God, could I use a good screwing to quiet my nerves, restore my confidence, and make me feel more like a woman than a burglar.

I covered his hand with mine and slowly moved it higher.

It would be corny to say Aaron played me like a fine violin, but I have to say that for a man who supposedly had had few opportunities for broad sexual experience, he did a damn good job of satisfying this woman, and from his expression as he withdrew and lay back on the bed, he was pretty satisfied as well.

As a distraction, it was a virtuoso performance.

Chapter 29

Neither of us had any trouble falling asleep following our little distraction. Six o'clock a.m. therefore arrived earlier than either Aaron or I wished it to, but the alarm clock beside the bed was insistent.

I yawned, looked over at a sleepy-but-satisfied-looking Aaron and said, "I'll get washed first; you can stay there for a while longer."

Aaron accepted the offer and turned over, closing his eyes and trying to catch just a few more z's. Meanwhile, I was humming softly as I discarded my nightgown in the bathroom and stepped into the shower. Once I'm up and functioning, I'm all business, and this was definitely a business day. High risk and high reward, just the kind of day that makes my adrenalin flow like a river at flood stage. Of course, I also needed a first cup of coffee to be truly human, but that would have to wait a while.

Ablutions completed, I donned bra and panties and covered those with a robe kindly supplied by the inn. Thus attired I went over to Aaron's side of the bed and sat down next to him. He seemed to have fallen asleep again, and I really hated to wake him, but time was of the essence and we didn't have much of it. So I leaned over and put my hand, warm from the shower, on his brow and stroked his forehead lightly until he opened his eyes.

"Wakey wakey," I said playfully. "Your turn in the bathroom. I've even left you some hot water."

Aaron started to protest, but he quickly realized I was right. "Okay," he said sleepily, "I know. There's work to do. And I don't want to be the reason we're late to the office."

Soon both of us were washed and dressed. A "continental breakfast" (muffins, orange juice, and coffee—I always wondered what continent these skimpy breakfasts referred to) had been left on a tray outside our door, and having finished that we turned our attention to Aaron's disguise, a false beard and moustache.

"I wish I'd practiced putting these on," he said, "because it seems to be a lot trickier than it looked." After several attempts that came out crooked or cockeyed and made him look like a horribly disfigured Mr. Potato Head, he turned to me for assistance.

"The trick is to line everything up and use plenty of that spirit gum stuff they gave you," I said. Together we managed to make Aaron's imitation facial hair look real enough to pass at least cursory inspection. I stepped back to view the finished product.

"Hmm, not bad," I said. "As long as no one gets too up close and personal, you should pass muster. But be sure you don't fiddle with them or they could come off, and wouldn't that be embarrassing?"

Aaron laughed. "Just embarrassing? More like incriminating." He held his hands up as if looking at a newspaper headline. "'Famous violinist caught burgling house in lousy disguise.'"

I cringed. That was exactly what I was afraid of.

****

Finally ready for action, I packed all our accessories into the Chevy. On its door I mounted the TidyHome sign I had purchased. Stepping back to admire the effect, I felt it would fool even the TidyHome girls themselves, should that become necessary. I waited until a few minutes after eight to make the necessary phone calls to TidyHome and Sanders, both of which seemed to go well, with no suspicion detectable in the other parties' voices.

I was feeling energized and optimistic, as I usually did before a job. This was, after all, what I had chosen to do with my life, and I had no regrets. Aaron, on the other hand, appeared to be suffering some understandable stage fright, together perhaps with a bout of what could be called a form of buyer's remorse: He had, in effect, purchased a burglary, complete with burglar, and he was about to find out whether it was a shrewd investment or a disastrous mistake. He was still game, however—and I'm sure his ego would never let him back out now after being so adamant about taking part. He presented a stiff, if recently redecorated, upper lip.

With all preparations accounted for, Aaron and I were finally ready for action. We had had to sneak out the rear door of the inn to avoid being seen by the proprietor, who would presumably not recognize Aaron in disguise and wonder what kind of *ménage a trois* Aaron and I were engaged in. In truth, it would have been unclear which was the worse disaster, Aaron being taken for a stranger and having to explain himself, or his being recognized for who he was and having to explain his disguise and then go back and do a better job of concealment.

As we drove, we talked about everything except the job ahead (and except what happened a few hours earlier). And regarding the job there wasn't much to say—either we were ready or we weren't.

I told Aaron my theory about burgling in the daytime in the fog and how I thought it had an advantage over burgling at night. He laughed, then said, "You know, there's another advantage, at least in Jewish law. You'll find it in Exodus, to be exact."

"Exodus talks about burgling in the fog?" I was more than a little skeptical.

"Absolutely. At least about burgling in the daytime. I learned this when I had my bar mitzvah, so it's a bit hazy, but as I recall, there's this long discussion of the punishments for various crimes, many of which were punishable by death."

"What kind of crimes?"

"Well, murder, of course. But also things like kidnapping, and even striking your parents. Anyway, it was considered justified to kill a burglar who entered your house at night, but not if he entered in the daytime."

"Really? Why?"

"I think it was because it was assumed someone who entered the house at night intended to harm the homeowner, or at least the homeowner was justified in thinking so."

"And a daytime burglar?"

"The daytime burglar, it was assumed, was just there to steal something. So the homeowner wasn't allowed to kill him."

Sounded good to me. "I guess, then, we fall into the daytime category," I said. "If we should get caught by Sanders, and it's still daytime, I hope he's up on his biblical studies."

And about then we arrived at our destination. Bible class over.

****

We turned onto La Paloma Road about 8:15 a.m. and parked in the same space in Little Hyde Park as Sara and I had occupied during our reconnaissance mission. There wasn't much fog in the air that morning, merely a light mist. I indicated the target and told Aaron how Sara and I had watched from that vantage point to see who went in and out, and when.

"We not only have to wait for Sanders to leave before going in, but we also have to be out of there before he gets back. We can't take a chance that he'll notice missing what his staff might not."

"When did you say he gets back?" Aaron asked.

"While we were watching, after four. But we can't assume he'll always be that late, so we have to be in and out as quickly as possible."

Aaron nodded agreement. But by 8:25 Sanders' black Mercedes hadn't made an appearance.

"I think we'd better make our move now," I said, "even if Sanders is still there. It'll look suspicious if the cleaners don't show up at about their usual time. And for all we know, Sanders isn't leaving today at all. So let's go."

Enter the faux cleaners, stage left.

****

I was driving, as I wanted to be the one speaking to the guard at the gate. I pulled the car up to the barrier and stopped. Immediately a young man in tan livery strode forward. I saw that his breast pocket bore the embroidered name "Jerry."

"Where are the usual cleaning ladies?" Jerry asked in a very pleasant, non-threatening tone, having glanced at the familiar sign on the car. I explained about the emergency back at the ranch and how I and Andy (the name I had arbitrarily chosen for Aaron—I was afraid his real first name might possibly trigger a clue to his real identity) had been pressed into service.

Jerry, apparently not the dimmest light in the marquee, maintained his pleasant tone but said, "I see. I hope you won't mind if I call up to the house, just to make sure it's okay. No one mentioned there'd be different ladies…I mean different people." He glanced at Aaron apologetically.

Uh oh, this might not be as simple as I hoped. Did whoever I spoke to forget to tell the rest of the staff? What if that person has left by now? But I just smiled and said, "Certainly, go ahead. I can understand your wanting to check."

"Thanks; just be a moment," Jerry said as he took out his cell phone and pressed a few keys. He spoke into the phone and then listened. The conversation was very brief, but for the few seconds it lasted I was just slightly anxious, and Aaron was probably trying hard not to wet his pants.

When Jerry hung up, however, he looked up and smiled at me to indicate all was well. "They said someone from the agency called earlier, but they forgot to tell me. Sorry for the delay. You can go right up." He stepped back and pushed a button on a small transmitter attached to his belt. The big iron gate swung back and the Chevy proceeded up the drive. To myself, I said, *I sure as hell hope every step along the way won't be this dicey.* But to Aaron I just smiled and said, "See? No problem. Everything's gonna be fine."

He looked like he wasn't so sure. But at least he still seemed to be dry.

****

We drove up to the big house, past tall rows of Japanese privet hedge on either side of the narrow road, then turned right at a circular driveway with lush plantings in the center that effectively hid the house behind it. I pulled the Chevy around to the side of the house, where it wouldn't be in the way, but where it was close enough to be handy in case we had to make a quick, unplanned exit. Aaron and I got out. I handed Aaron the keys, which he put in his pocket—my uniform didn't have pockets to speak of. We went around to the rear of the car and opened the trunk, from which we took the custom carrier, filled with cleaning products on top and concealing Aaron's replica Guarneri in its lower compartment. Aaron carried it, as it was quite heavy and somewhat bulky.

"What are you looking at?" Aaron asked. I had paused and was staring at the left side of the house, which consisted of a blank wall except for a single door in about the middle.

"Nothing, I guess," I said. "I was trying to compare my recollection of the floor plan Rafael sent us with what I'm actually seeing. Let's go on in."

As we approached the front door, we both stopped to stare up at the impressive façade, two stories high, a blend of orderly Edwardian and ornate Victorian architecture. The body color was white, with a pretty marine blue trim. The surrounding plantings were impeccable. Three wide steps led us up to a shallow wrap-around porch and a massive front door, in which was set an oval leaded-glass window.

I took a deep breath and turned to Aaron.

"This is it. Let's go."

I rang the bell.

Chapter 30

Soon the door was opened by a very attractive, well-scrubbed young woman—well, young by my standards, but probably about thirty—with what you'd call a winning smile. She was wearing a maid's uniform that was a bit less revealing than the one I had rented, though it was filled out quite nicely with ample breasts and a sculptured derriere. I noticed that Aaron's eyes had wandered to both these features almost immediately. I couldn't really blame him.

"Hi," she said. "I'm Marianne, Mr. Sanders' housekeeper. C'mon in." Her voice was soft and friendly, sounding as if she was glad to see us. She stepped aside and we entered. Passing through a small foyer, we stepped into a large and brightly lit living room.

Aaron and I surveyed our surroundings. Through the tall front windows, we could see the garden we had passed through on our way in. Beyond the garden the narrow lane leading up from La Paloma Road was just visible, and beyond that the trees that mostly concealed Little Hyde Park.

The room itself was quite revealing. If we hadn't already known that Sanders was a very wealthy man, the size of the room, the quality of the furnishings, and the nature of the artwork on the walls and surfaces would have made that fact quite clear. This was the living room of a man who lived well, entertained in style, collected fine things, and liked to display what he collected.

Possibly including Marianne.

Speaking of whom, Marianne turned to me and said, "Mr. Sanders says you're substituting for the regular gals. What happened?"

"Oh, one of our big clients had some kind of emergency," I said, "and they needed extra help. Your regular cleaners were called in, and I guess it took longer than they expected, 'cause they called me and said if I had the time they needed me to come do your place."

"Aren't you one of their regular gals?"

"No, I usually work on my own. I used to work for TidyHome, and so I still fill in sometimes when they need me." *It's going over pretty good. Even I might believe it.*

"So what's your name?"

"Frances," I said. I'd almost used my real name, but stopped myself just in time. No use giving away more of one's identity than necessary.

Marianne smiled and nodded, then turned toward Aaron, who had been hanging back, hoping to fade into the woodwork, I suppose.

Not a chance. "And who's this?" Marianne asked. "You don't look like a housemaid to me." She gave Aaron a bright smile.

"Oh, that's Andy," I said when Aaron seemed unlikely to respond. "He usually works on big cleanup jobs, you know, like after a fire or flood, but he agreed to come along today to help me out."

"Andy" smiled and nodded in agreement.

Marianne seemed to think this over, then she said to Aaron, "Hmmm. Why didn't they just call you two out for that big emergency job they had, instead of our usual girls?" It was a reasonable question. Marianne, who was obviously a sharp lady, was probably just making conversation, trying to be friendly and put us newcomers at our ease. But of course her small talk was having just the opposite effect on me and, especially, Aaron.

I could see that Aaron was getting flustered by being put on the spot like this, and I was afraid he might say something we'd regret. What's more, I couldn't believe that I hadn't thought of this particular question, much less an answer for it, beforehand. And I had only a few seconds to come up with that answer now.

"Oh, well, Aar…I mean Andy was out of town until this morning, so he missed their call about the emergency. Just got back when they called him about helping me with this job. Right, Andy?"

Aaron nodded in agreement. "Right. Yeah, that's exactly right. Missed the call. I mean the first call. That is—"

I jumped back in before Aaron could make things any worse. I stepped in front of Marianne and, with a broad smile, asked, "So where do we start?"

But before Marianne could answer, two men walked into the living room from the hallway beyond. One was large, muscular, and thoroughly unpleasant-looking. If you can picture one of those ex-prize fighters in the movies who had taken one too many punches in his time, that pretty well described the man. My immediate reaction was that I wouldn't want to meet him in a dark alley. Or even a light one.

The other man, however, was the total opposite, and it was he who smiled and extended his hand first to me, then to Aaron, who was standing behind me trying to look inconspicuous.

"How do you do"? the man said. "I'm Jim Sanders. I see you've met Marianne." As he said this, he reached around and patted Marianne, who was just within range, on the tush. I found the gesture both offensive and revealing at the same time.

Marianne, however, didn't seem to take notice, which was also revealing. I assumed she was much more than Sanders' housekeeper, if you get my drift.

Sanders was a man of about sixty years old, with close-cropped hair that could be either blond or light gray. He was clean-shaven and his well-tanned and almost wrinkle-free face gave off a healthy glow: a fine candidate for an after-shave lotion commercial. Clearly this man kept himself in good condition.

He flashed a very white smile and said, "I guess you're the substitute cleaning crew. Well, I won't be in the way. I'm just running a little late this morning. I leave you in good hands: Marianne really runs the place." He winked in her direction.

He started to move toward the door, the prizefighter following behind, when he stopped and turned back. Addressing me and gesturing to the big man, he said, "Oh, I'm sorry. This is Benny. He's kind of a combination chauffeur, handyman, and bodyguard." Benny nodded in our direction, but it was not a friendly nod. Benny probably dispensed smiles as often as the Pope dispensed crack cocaine. "Benny'll be back after he takes me into town, so if there's anything you need, he'll be available to get it for you. Otherwise I'm sure Marianne will show you where everything is."

Sanders and Benny made their way to the door. As Benny passed me, I could see a distinct bulge in his jacket where no anatomical parts were located. Benny was carrying.

I wondered why a grocery magnate might need a bodyguard. But then I realized that although a grocer might not, an art thief just might.

When Sanders and Benny were finally driving away, I again asked Marianne where we should start our cleaning.

"Start? Oh, it doesn't really matter. The whole house needs cleaning, so you might as well start here and work your way 'round. You'll find the cleaning supplies in that cupboard over there," she said, pointing to a closet in the hallway. "Just call me if you have any questions. I'll be doing the laundry, then getting lunch ready in the kitchen." And she left us cleaners on our own.

"Geez, that was a close one," Aaron said *sotto voce*. "Thanks for getting me off the hook."

"That's okay. It's always the unexpected you have to watch out for, whether it's a question or an alarm or a dog."

"So what do we do now?"

"Just like we planned. We clean the house, work our way around to the gallery, hope the violin is there, if so take it and get the hell out."

Aaron didn't ask the obvious next question—what if it wasn't there—but gave a silent salute and headed for the cupboard that Marianne had indicated.

****

It took us intrepid housecleaners about three hours to make our way around the living quarters. I had told Aaron to keep an eye out for anything that might be a clue to either the murder weapon or the violin's location, our twin objectives, which slowed us down a bit. Aaron turned out to be a pretty good cleaner, which I should have guessed from my own observation of how neat his hotel room was. He actually seemed to be enjoying himself as he dusted, vacuumed, and polished. To me, of course, having cleaned houses for a living before changing to my current profession, it was familiar territory.

We didn't come across Aaron's violin while we were cleaning the main part of the house, despite quite a bit of snooping in cupboards and closets as we went. We did, however, find something of great interest with respect to Martin's killer. About an hour into the job, Aaron held up a piece of paper he had found when emptying a waste basket.

"Take a look at this," he said with some excitement. Someone had begun what looked like the text for a "lost and found" notice, as might go in the newspaper or online, written in pencil. It read:

Lost: Man's ring, initials BJD. Reward. Phone 4

"Looks like someone was going to advertise for that ring and changed their mind," I said. "What was that chauffeur's name again?"

"Bennie, I think. Didn't get his last name."

"I'll bet it starts with 'D'," I said. "I think we're one big step closer to our objective, or at least mine." I put the paper in my pocket and we resumed cleaning.

Just before noon, "Andy" and I reached the entrance to what I assumed, from Rafael's description of the house, was the gallery in which I hoped we'd find the Guarneri. The door was closed, and it had an impressive-looking lock, but when I turned the handle, the door opened. I wouldn't have to spend any time or risk getting caught picking the lock. Just then, a familiar voice behind me called out, "Excuse me. Frances?"

It took a moment before I realized that I was Frances. I turned around to face a smiling Marianne.

"We were just going to start on this next room," I said, trying to sound casual.

"My fault," she said, "I forgot to tell you that room's kind of private. You don't have to clean in there."

But I want to clean in there, I wanted to say, but instead I just nodded and said, "Yes, ma'am. We'll move on." What else could I do?

Marianne seemed pleased. "Great. Oh, and I wanted to know whether you two want some lunch. It's about noon and I'm fixing sandwiches for me and the guys," which I took to mean Jerry the guard and Benny. At least I hoped there weren't any more "guys" lurking around. "Would you like some while I'm at it?"

In truth, I was hungry and would have loved one of those sandwiches, and I'm sure Aaron was likewise. But we were on the verge of entering the gallery, the very room we had come to see (and burgle), so with reluctance I declined, saying, "That's really sweet of you, Marianne, but I think we'll keep on working until we're done. Thanks for asking, though."

"No problem," Marianne responded, "if you need anything, we'll be eating lunch in the kitchen." She turned and headed back in that direction.

"So what do we do now?" Aaron whispered.

"We go in there, of course," I said, indicating the gallery door. "The longer we spend here, the more chance she'll be back or something else will go wrong."

We hurriedly picked up our tools and entered the gallery.

Chapter 31

It was dark in the gallery. There appeared to be no windows to bring in natural light (and possibly fade priceless masterpieces), and only one door, the door we had entered. I found a light switch and flipped it up. Soft lighting bathed the edges of the ceiling and highlighted a beautiful display of artwork on the walls. Another switch illuminated the floor area containing various free-standing sculptures and other *objets d'art*, with single beams from ceiling-mounted spotlights. The light was not very bright, but it was sufficient to see around the room. From the low whistle he gave, I could tell that Aaron, despite the fact that he was probably used to being in elegant surroundings, was clearly impressed.

It was my hope that Sanders would want to put his new acquisition on display, even if he planned later to swap it for a painting. And if this gallery, which obviously was not open to just any visitor to the house, contained at least some of his "private" collection, Aaron's Guarneri might be here. But if it was, we'd have to find it in a hurry.

Aaron was gazing at the remarkable display, but I was concentrating on only one thing: Is the Guarneri there? If it wasn't, then finding it was going to be a very difficult proposition.

If it was there, it obviously would be among the

objects on the floor. The door where we entered was located in about the center of the room, and the sculptures and such were displayed in an oval pattern, so one could walk clockwise around the perimeter and view the paintings on the walls to the left and the sculptures, etc. to the right. Or vice versa, of course, depending on which direction one chose to walk.

I left Aaron to watch the door, listening for an approaching intruder, and then started walking hurriedly to my left and quickly made my way around the gallery, examining the objects as I went. Halfway around I paused to check out something I saw on the wall, then I continued until I had made it almost completely around, with no violin in sight. I was beginning to lose hope, when there it was, almost the last object in line: what I was certain was Aaron's beloved Guarneri, on display on an elegant wooden stand clearly made especially for it.

I ran up to Aaron and took his arm, pointing him in the direction of the violin display. When he saw what I was indicating, he suddenly looked faint. I'm sure that at that moment, all the emotions that he had experienced since his violin was stolen—the shock of its loss, the anger at the man who he learned had stolen it, the determination to get it back, the hope for recovery offered by finding a burglar in his suite, the stress of planning to recover it, the intervening murder of Donny Martin, and finally the fear and anxiety accompanying carrying out the plan—were momentarily replaced by the elation of suddenly being so close to having it back.

He put down the tools he was carrying and started to walk toward the violin display, but I grabbed his arm and stopped him.

"No, I'll go. You stay here at the door and warn me if anyone's coming." I actually had no idea what we would do if anyone did find us there after being told not to enter. Plead a very short memory? At least disobeying cleaning orders shouldn't be a capital offense.

"Why can't I go and you stay?" Aaron pleaded.

"Because it's not that easy. These things on display are all fastened down in some way, and I'm sure your violin is too. You won't know how to get it free and substitute the copy without it being noticeable."

Aaron looked back through the open door, where one could just see down the hallway toward the kitchen, and then at his violin, which I know he dearly wished to rescue himself, and finally relented.

"Okay, you go get it and I'll watch. But hurry."

Don't worry, I lost no time. I grabbed the custom wooden carrier, now somewhat lighter with the cleaning equipment removed, and almost sprinted to Aaron's violin. I stopped next to the display stand that proudly supported a violin that looked, to me at least, like the one that I had first attempted to steal in Aaron's hotel suite.

I bent down and extracted from the hidden compartment in the carrier that very violin, the one I had been holding when Aaron walked in on me.

I laid the copy down on the floor, glancing up to see if Aaron was watching me or the door. He was watching the door. As I had expected, the violin on the display stand was attached to it by a length of multi-strand cable looped around the neck and in front of the pegs, so that it could not be slipped off past the scroll on the end. The other end was inserted into a sheath that covered the vertical arm of the stand itself. It was a clever design that left only a small length of cable and the loop around the violin to be seen. Fortunately, there didn't seem to be an alarm connected to the cable, something that would have slowed me down considerably.

I had come prepared, and I took from the carrier a set of wire cutters. When I tried to cut the cable with them, however, I found they couldn't penetrate its surface. Whatever the metal of the sheath was, it was tougher than that of the cutters.

I again looked up at Aaron, and he was giving me a "hurry up" sign. Either he was just antsy, or someone was headed our way. In either case, I knew there was no time to waste. I had anticipated the possibility of needing something stronger to cut the cable, but I had hesitated to bring heavy-duty cable cutters because of their weight and bulk. Now I was glad I had. I reached into the top compartment of the carrier and brought out an instrument that looked as if it could sever the cables holding up the Golden Gate Bridge. Although that might exceed its abilities, the small cable around the Guarneri did not. The only problem was to avoid damaging the violin with its oversized jaws. I carefully placed the front of the jaws over the loop and, pressing one handle against my chest and holding the other, closed the jaws on the cable.

At least I tried to close them. The awkward way I was operating the cutter gave me very little leverage, and even though a clever ratchet system greatly reduced the effort needed to operate the cutters, I couldn't gain enough force to cut the cable. Looking up again at

Aaron, I saw that he was looking very agitated, and his "hurry up" signal had changed to a frantic "what the hell are you doing." I ignored him. With the jaws of the cutter now holding the cable in place, I slowly slid my free hand down to the handle that was pressing into my chest. When I had it in hand, I pushed the two handles together as hard as I could. Finally I heard a satisfying "snap" as the cutters overcame the cable's resistance and opened the loop holding the violin.

As quickly as I safely could, I freed the violin from the cable and lifted it off the display stand. I put it aside, then picked up the replica we had brought and placed it on the stand in exactly the same place. I put the loop of cable around the neck of the substitute violin, then took out a small tube of super glue. I applied a dab to the cut ends of the loop, held them together for a few seconds, then stepped back to view my work. Only on close inspection would anyone notice that the loop had been cut and repaired, or for that matter that the violin on the stand was not the same one that had been there five minutes earlier.

I was proud of my handiwork, but I didn't have much time to admire it.

"Someone's coming," Aaron called out. I threw the cable cutters into the top of my carrier and reached for Aaron's violin to slide it into the secret compartment.

That was when disaster struck.

In my haste—okay, panic—I tripped over the carrier just as I reached for the violin. After a horrible few seconds of trying to regain my balance, I not only knocked the substitute violin off the display I had so carefully fashioned, but I came crashing down on top of the violin I had just liberated.

Apart from the noise this made—and it made plenty as I knocked over two other displays on my way down—it probably gave Aaron the closest thing to a heart attack he'll ever have. He came rushing over to see what damage had been done—I'd like to think to me as well as the Guarneri, but I'm a realist. He picked me up, and then picked up the violin that lay beneath me.

It was a total loss, the neck broken and the body splintered. At that moment I wished it was my neck that was broken, but no such luck. As we gazed down at what had been a violin, we again simultaneously uttered the familiar three words that had first introduced us:

"It's a fake!"

We both were staring at the inside of the broken instrument that, like the one we had brought with us, was missing that all-important label. Only in this case, it was not even a very good copy, except perhaps to a dummy like me in very dim light. I assume Sanders, awaiting the theft of the Guarneri, had acquired a cheap copy as a placeholder in the display he'd arranged until he had possession of the real one. Of course, at this point all that counted was that it wasn't Aaron's violin that got crushed.

Unfortunately, we hadn't time to enjoy this reprieve before Benny entered the room, took one look at us amid a tangle of strings, cables, and burglar tools, and drew out his pistol.

****

To say this was an unexpected development would be somewhat of an understatement. It was about the worst combination of circumstances I could have imagined. Maybe even beyond my imagination.

Strangely, it flashed through my mind that at least we knew for sure who had shot Donny Martin—Benny. And at least I hadn't crushed a priceless Guarneri. Small comforts now.

Benny, surprisingly, didn't look particularly angry. In fact, he had something of a smirk on his face, as if to say, "Look what I found. I'll probably get a nice bonus from the boss." To me, that smirk was far more terrifying than had he simply been angry. Either way I didn't give us much chance of survival.

Benny stepped around us, his smirk having become more of a grin. He was clearly enjoying himself. He gestured toward the door and said, "That way." We obeyed, stepping over the wreckage of the ersatz Guarneri and backing up in the direction of the door.

Then an unexpected thing happened: Benny, perhaps enjoying himself too much, didn't look where he was going and tripped over the tangle of wood and wire we had left on the floor. He pitched forward with a loud scream and fell heavily to the floor. As his hand hit the hard floor, his gun was propelled several feet in our direction. Aaron and I both scrambled for it, Aaron winning the contest and picking it up.

So there we were, gun in hand and trained on Benny. I couldn't believe our luck.

Aaron was ecstatic. "We may not have the violin," he said to me, "but we can clear you with the police. I'll bet anything this is the gun that killed Martin and Fred Ballard."

Before I could respond, we were interrupted by a voice behind us.

"I'll take that bet."

Chapter 32

We both turned around, slowly. We didn't really want to see what was there but had no choice.

What was there was Marianne, only this time she was not smiling. And the weapon she was holding in her hand, despite its small size, looked more than capable of doing lethal damage. I assume she was carrying it in one of those under-bra holsters I've read about, because she hadn't any suspicious bulges on her svelte figure last I saw her.

"I don't know who took out Ballard," she said, "but this little baby sent off that chiseler Martin when he tried to blackmail Mr. Sanders, and it'll do the same for you two if you make one false move."

Maybe it was my imagination, but Marianne's voice seemed to have lost that soft sweetness it had when we came in.

Marianne's revelation, or confession, had caught me totally by surprise. It also made that little weapon she was pointing at us seem as threatening as if it were an assault rifle. As inconspicuously as possible, given the state of my nerves, I brought my right hand over to my left wrist and pressed what I hoped was the record button on my new watch. Marianne saw me and said, "Hey, keep your hands where I can see them!"

"Sorry." Now I needed a reprise of Marianne's admission.

I managed to say, shakily, "You mean you…you shot Martin?"

"Had to. I went up there to get the violin, ready to pay what Mr. Sanders promised. The little bastard said he didn't have it, that his roommate Ballard had taken it and disappeared. Then he had the balls to demand I give him the money anyway or he'd expose Mr. Sanders', uh, methods. You might say I then made an executive decision."

She smiled. It wasn't pretty.

Benny, who had by now recovered his composure and his pistol, made his way over to Marianne's side.

"What d'ya think these two were up to?" he asked.

"I'm not entirely sure," Marianne said. "It looks like theft, but that doesn't explain their knowing about Martin and Ballard."

She pointed her pistol in my direction and said, "Okay Frances, or whatever your real name is, what the hell's going on here? Who sent you, and what's your connection to Donny Martin?"

When I didn't immediately respond, having nothing helpful to say (helpful to me, at least), Benny piped up:

"I bet I can get an answer out of her." He almost sounded hopeful that she would let him try.

You can bet that sent the wrong message to my bladder.

"Never mind," Marianne said. "It's not our decision what to do with them, it's Mr. Sanders'. He'll be home pretty soon, so we've just got to keep 'em on ice until he gets here and tells us what to do." It was clear Marianne was in command regarding things that took place within the four walls of Chez Sanders, because Benny didn't protest. And certainly neither Aaron nor I was going to argue with Marianne's decision.

"We could call the police," Benny offered meekly. He didn't relish waiting around when action of some kind seemed called for.

Marianne shook her head. "I told you we'll wait for Mr. Sanders. You know he doesn't like dealing with the police and having them snooping around here. Remember that time someone stole one of the cars?"

"Oh yeah, I remember," Benny said, rolling his eyes a bit. "He wouldn't let you call the police or nothin'. I had t' go out lookin' for the damn car myself. Took me two days to find it and those assholes who stole it." Suddenly he smiled, in a menacing sort of way. "Bet they wished the police had found 'em first."

I didn't want to think about why the car thieves might have preferred the police.

More to herself than any of us, Marianne added, "Besides, they can connect us, including Mr. Sanders, with Martin's little, uh, accident. We wouldn't want the police hearing about that, would we?"

"So what do we do with 'em while we wait for Mr. Sanders?" Benny asked.

Marianne gave this some thought before replying, "Let's lock 'em here in the gallery. It hasn't any windows, and the door locks tight, so they'll be sure to still be there when Mr. Sanders gets back. Meanwhile, I'll see if I can get hold of him on his cell phone, so this won't be a surprise to him when he gets home.

"He doesn't like surprises."

****

Benny made a quick check for weapons, patting

Aaron's pockets. There was only one small pocket in my tight-fitting maid's uniform, from which he extracted my small cell phone, which I had brought along in a belt-and-suspenders spirit. Now only the suspenders were left. He found no suspicious bulges; fortunately, he refrained from patting down those that were obviously anatomical. He did, however, take the car keys out of Aaron's pocket.

"Should I take their watches?" Benny asked Marianne.

"Why, you need a watch?" Marianne replied in a sarcastic tone. "They wanna know the time, it's fine with me."

"When did you say you expect the boss home?" Benny asked.

"Come to think of it, he said he'd be a little late today, maybe about seven."

"That must be why he had me come on home with the car, said he'd take a cab home. But that's okay. They'll keep."

Then his face sort of lit up and he said to Marianne, "I got an idea. Go get those handcuffs I won playin' poker last year. They're in the top drawer of that chest in the shop. We may finally have a use for 'em."

"Good idea." And she went out the front door, returning a few minutes later with a pair of very official-looking handcuffs. Benny must have been playing poker with a policeman or private detective. I guessed if things like deeds and bonds and even houses could end up as stakes in poker games, as I knew all had at one time or another, why not a pair of handcuffs?

Marianne left Benny to his task, muttering almost to herself as she left the gallery, "Too bad. Best damn cleaning job we've had." I guess I was flattered.

Benny looked around the gallery for a place to anchor his prisoners. He finally settled on one right there by the door, a very heavy bronze sculpture in the shape of some Greek god or other. He put one cuff on my wrist, passed the other through the cable that secured the sculpture to its base, and closed that cuff on Aaron's wrist.

As Benny was about to leave, I just had to ask a question that had been bugging me since we learned that Marianne, not Benny or any other man, was the one who killed Martin.

"Benny," I said, "would you mind clearing up just one thing for me: Who the hell is BJD?"

Benny paused and scratched his head. "BJD . . . oh yeah, BJD. How d'ya know about him?"

"It's a long story. Who is he?"

"Oh, he's Marianne's fiancé. She used to wear his ring 'round her neck, you know, on a chain, like some women do? Apparently the chain broke somewhere an' she lost the ring. Has no idea where. Real upset, she was. You shoulda heard the language." He actually chuckled. "She c'n swear better'n I can."

"She certainly leads a busy life." I refrained from revealing where Marianne had lost her ring, seeing no benefit and a possible downside if I did. Dire as our circumstances were, I was pleased that little mystery—who dropped the ring and how it ended up next to Martin's body—was cleared up. Marianne probably broke the chain when she extracted her lethal little weapon from her bodice in order to shoot Martin. I could understand how she might've been distracted under the circumstances.

His momentary better mood dissipated, Benny turned off the lights, closed and locked the door, and left Aaron and me alone in the gallery.

We were in what was doubtless the world's most elegant prison.

Chapter 33

It was pitch dark. (Kind of like a closet I'd been in recently.) Fortunately, the light switch was within my reach and, after a few tries, I found the switch that lit only the corners of the ceiling, enough light to see but not enough to show under the door. Better that our jailers thought we were sitting in the dark, contemplating our sins.

Aaron was the first to speak, in a low and very unhappy voice.

"I'm really sorry, Flo. I guess this wouldn't've happened if you'd been on your own."

"Shh! I'm the one who should apologize. If I'm so professional, why didn't I watch where I was going? Anyway, it's too late for that. The fact is that we may be in much better shape than you think, or than we could've hoped for."

"Whattaya mean? It looks pretty hopeless to me."

"Listen. Remember me checking the side of the house when we arrived?"

"Sure."

"Well, I noticed an inconspicuous door in the middle of the outside wall that didn't show up on the plan Rafael sent us, right about where the gallery would be. That means there may be a way out from the gallery that's not apparent from the inside, or there's another room Rafael didn't know about. We cleaned the entire house and didn't come across such a room. I'm hoping that means there's some hidden connection between the gallery and outside, perhaps for bringing in large objects."

"Or stolen objects," Aaron said. "Or maybe it's just a storage closet."

I preferred not to consider that possibility.

"So how do we get to this escape hatch?' Aaron asked. "It obviously doesn't open into this room."

"Maybe it does," I said. "While I was making the rounds of the treasures here, I was also looking for some evidence of a concealed opening in what would be the outside wall," indicating with a nod of my head the far wall. "I think I found one."

Aaron looked over at the far wall, which I'm sure looked pretty solid to him, and nodded, but he still didn't look very happy. "Okay, so let's say there's a door there. Even if there were some way to get through it, how are we going to do it now, with these?" He looked down at the handcuffs, which appeared pretty solid.

"We're going to get through it the same way we're going to get out of these damn handcuffs, by using these." Turning away modestly (a seemingly unnecessary gesture considering the recent past), I extracted from inside the low-cut blouse of my uniform and between my breasts the small locksmith tools I used to enter strange houses. Turning back to Aaron, I said, "Luckily, those two didn't bother to check for hidden stuff like this. Pretty careless of them, but they probably aren't used to frisking prisoners."

Aaron looked more than a little relieved to see the tools. He laughed and asked, "The benefits of cleavage.

What else have you got hidden in there?" I just smiled, and a few minutes later we were both free of the cuffs, rubbing our wrists where the metal had bruised them.

"Okay so far," Aaron said. "Now if I understand, you're going to find this hidden door, open it with your doohickey there, and we leave by the back door you saw. Sounds like the plot of a Nancy Drew mystery."

I was intrigued. "How do you know about Nancy Drew? I thought only us girls read her."

"My sister. Had the whole set, I think. Read a few to me. Lots of hidden rooms and stairways and such."

"Well good, just call me Nancy and watch me solve the Mystery of the Purloined Violin."

Unfortunately, my little joke served as a painful reminder to Aaron that even if we succeeded in saving our skins, we would have failed in our original mission, finding and recovering his violin.

"I'm really sorry about that," I told him. "I did the best I could."

"Not your fault," he said. "You warned me there was a good chance we'd fail, and I can see now that without you, that chance of failure would've been more like a hundred percent."

Unfortunately, I couldn't disagree, so I left it there.

****

We moved slowly around to the other side of the gallery and the middle of the far wall, where I had seen the concealed door.

"How will you find it, much less open it, in this light?" Aaron asked. The soft ceiling illumination was far too dim for close work.

I put my finger to my lips to summon silence, then I extracted an object about the size of a thin book of matches from behind the waistband of my short skirt. I squeezed the object between thumb and forefinger and a narrow beam of light shot from one edge. I then examined the center of the wall closely until I found the outline of the door I had noticed on my earlier perusal. A further inspection revealed a small keyhole hidden behind a painting of a lazy river with a grove of trees on its bank, probably by one of the French impressionists whose name I had no time to discover. I moved the painting to one side, sliding it along on the hangers behind it.

"Hold this," I whispered to Aaron, handing him the tiny flashlight, "so I can use both hands on this lock. And listen for anyone coming."

Aaron took the object as ordered, squeezing it and aiming it at the lock I had found. Meanwhile I selected one of the tools from my mini-pick kit and inserted it into the lock. I had no sooner begun to work the tool into position when Aaron whispered, "Someone's coming!"

"Quick, get back where we were!"

I pulled the pick out of the lock, shoved the picture more or less back to center, and almost dove headfirst for the place by the door where we had been secured, pulling Aaron after me and flicking off the lights.

Immediately came the sound of the door being unlocked, then opened. Marianne took a step into the gallery, reached over to the wall and turned on the main lights. She looked over at the two figures huddled around the Greek statue, apparently bereft and defeated.

"Just making sure you folks are comfortable. I talked with Mr. Sanders, and he's mad as hell about you two. I imagine you're gonna wish you'd only end up in jail." She smiled unpleasantly.

Satisfied that we weren't going anywhere carrying a thousand-pound sculpture, she turned out the light, locking the door behind her. She didn't bother to turn off the low light I had turned on earlier, so there was still a bit of illumination in the room.

As soon as I heard the click of the lock, I sprang up. I motioned to Aaron to follow and together we made our way back to the hidden door. "She probably won't be back for at least a little while," I whispered, "so let's get this over with." Once again I pushed the picture aside and began to work on the lock.

As I worked, Aaron looked on with admiration. He whispered, "Someday you'll have to teach me how you do that."

I didn't look up from my work, but I did whisper back, "Someday. Not today. Besides, I hope you aren't planning to make a career of this sort of thing."

Five minutes and a good measure of muttered profanity later, I finally felt the lock's cylinder surrender and turn. I stepped back. The door was unlocked, but how was I supposed to open it? I pushed against it, but it didn't budge. Apparently it was intended to be opened outward, with the turned key itself the only available "handle" with which to pull it out.

I didn't have the key, of course. I stepped farther back and looked at the wall for a minute. All I needed was something attached to the door in the area of the lock (which would be opposite the side with the hinges) that could be pulled outward and bring the door with it. Meanwhile, Aaron held the flashlight and whispered, "Why are you staring at the wall and not trying to open the door?" I wasn't staring; I was thinking.

Then I saw a possible solution. I reached up and carefully took down the impressionist painting, which on closer inspection turned out to be by Manet, revealing behind it two heavy-duty picture hooks firmly attached to the wall just above the lock. In hanging the painting there in order to conceal the lock, it was possible Sanders had inadvertently provided us with just the handle we needed.

I very gently set the painting on the floor, leaning against the wall. It was much heavier than I had expected and might well be worth as much as the Guarneri for all I knew. I then examined the picture hooks to decide whether they were up to the task I had in mind for them. Of this I was unsure. They would have to be pulled gently, to be sure they stayed in the wall.

A second problem would be how to pull them at all. I tried to grip the hangers, but they slipped out of my fingers when I pulled on them. I stepped back and again studied the situation. Then I extracted two of the thin lock picks I had used earlier and gave one to Aaron, who by now had figured out the problem I was wrestling with. I whispered, "You're stronger than I am. Take this and slip it sideways into the hook on the bottom of the hanger closest to the lock. I'll go over to the edge of the door. If you can just get the door pulled out a half inch or so, maybe I can get it the rest of the way. But be careful not to pull the hanger out."

Aaron nodded and took the proffered tool. I found the leading edge of the door, which I knew had to be the side near the lock, and waited.

Aaron placed the thin pick horizontally into the "v"

of the hanger. He pulled down and out, but nothing happened. He tried several more times, but he simply couldn't get a sufficient grip on either the hook or the little lock pick.

"What I need is something to hold onto," he whispered. I looked around at the near-dark room and could see nothing useful. Aaron also looked around, and suddenly his eyes fell on a familiar object. As I watched, he made his way over to one of the exhibits, again holding the little flashlight. His back was to me and I couldn't tell what he was doing, but two minutes later he returned with a triumphant look on his face and something in his hand.

"Voila!" he whispered, showing me what he was holding. It looked at first like a thick piece of twine, but on closer inspection it turned out to be a very different kind of string: a violin string—two of them, in fact. Aaron had taken them off the violin that we—okay, I— had earlier destroyed.

A violin string does not make a perfect door pull by any means, but with some effort Aaron managed to hook the strings onto the picture hangers. He now had the leverage and the hold he needed to put some weight behind his effort to pull the door outward. He got just sufficient outward force to bring the piece of the wall that formed the door a fraction of an inch out of its resting place. This enabled me, using my lock pick and my fingernails, to help work it a bit farther until I was able to grip the edge with my fingers and, as Aaron continued to pull, work the door clear of the surrounding wall. At that point I could get my hand behind it, and a few seconds later it was open and beckoning for us to go through.

Aaron and I peered from the near-darkness of the gallery into the total darkness beyond the door. But we didn't need any light to realize this door did not lead to the outside and freedom, but to another room. Never mind, any room was preferable to the one we were leaving. After a moment's hesitation, I stepped through the opening.

Aaron looked back at the locked door through which Marianne or, worse, Benny might come at any moment, then followed me into the darkness.

Chapter 34

"Close the door behind you," I whispered back to Aaron.

I had been wondering how he was going to do that, considering the trouble we had had opening it, but I was pleased to find that there was an actual handle on the inside of the secret door, as well as a thumb-turn for the lock. After all, there was no need to hide the door or its hardware from anyone who was already in the room. Aaron pulled, and the door swung shut. Then he seemed to have a sudden change of heart and hurriedly reopened the door and stepped back into the gallery.

Observing this strange behavior, I didn't know what to make of it—surely Aaron was not planning to retreat just when victory was in sight—until he stepped back into the dark room and again closed the door.

"What was that all about?" I whispered.

"Re-hung the painting on the door. If they come in and find us gone, they won't immediately see that we're in here."

I looked at Aaron in a new light. I was impressed. He was starting to show the instincts of a fine burglar.

"Good for you," I said. "I should've thought of that myself. We may have to raise your status from 'dangerous amateur' to 'promising apprentice'."

If Aaron blushed at this faint praise, it was too dark for me to tell.

I turned the lock and breathed a little sigh of relief. Then I asked Aaron for my little flashlight, which was still in his pocket. "Stay here," I told him, "while I look around a bit."

I shined the narrow beam around our immediate surroundings and found that we were standing in a narrow aisle connecting the gallery wall door with the center of what appeared to be a windowless workroom, the length of the gallery and maybe eight feet wide. On our left was some kind of workbench, on our right a table and cabinets. As I moved forward, I could see that the room was a long rectangle, and I was crossing its narrow dimension at about the center. In front of me I thought I saw the door I had mentioned to Aaron, although the flashlight beam was too weak to cast much light on that far wall.

Turning left into the center aisle and feeling my way so as not to bump into any sharp objects, I directed the flashlight toward the top of the workbench on my left. Almost the first thing the light landed on caused me a sharp intake of breath. There on the bench, lying peacefully on a large piece of red velvet, was a beautiful old violin. Although it looked very much like the one I had almost stolen from Aaron's suite, as well as the one I had mistakenly tried to steal from the Sanders gallery an hour or so earlier, I was somehow certain that the instrument beneath my flashlight's beam must be the real thing.

Of course, this time I was not going to assume I was correct. This time I had brought along an invaluable accessory, the world's foremost expert on the authenticity of this particular violin. I made my way back to where Aaron was still standing by the gallery door, took his hand in mine, and slowly led him around to where I had found the violin. His violin, I fervently hoped.

As we approached the front of the workbench, my heart raced and I began to perspire. I suddenly realized clearly, for the first time since the adventure had begun, that I was not just hoping that this was the real violin because it would lead to a hundred thousand dollar payoff, more than I had ever made from a single job, lawful or unlawful. Nor was it because I could finally be done with this escapade that I had never really wanted to begin. No, I was hoping even more fervently that Aaron, who wanted so badly to recover his treasure from the man who had taken it from him that he was willing to risk his career, if not his life, for it, would finally see that desire realized.

We stopped in front of the workbench and again I trained the beam of my flashlight on the object in repose on its bed of velvet. As soon as I did I heard a small gasp behind me as Aaron reached out and picked up the violin. I handed him the flashlight so he could examine it as carefully as he wished. He first ran the beam of light slowly over the violin's top, then along its sides and back. Finally he peered inside at the all-important label. When he was finished, he handed the flashlight back to me.

I couldn't see Aaron's face, so I didn't know whether it displayed a look of triumph or disappointment.

"Well?" I whispered. "Is this the one?"

Aaron leaned over and kissed me lightly on the forehead. "You've done it," he said. "You've found my violin."

Chapter 35

Although I was elated that we had finally found Aaron's Guarneri, I was well aware that we were far from home free. In fact, we were far from both home and being free of our captivity. That was the next order of business.

I knew we had very limited time in which to leave the Sanders house with both our violin and our freedom. Not only would Sanders be coming home sometime soon, but at any moment Benny or Marianne might come to check on us again.

I turned and whispered to Aaron, who was holding his violin almost reverentially. I had to tap him on the arm to get his attention.

"Look, we've gotta get out of here right now. I'll take care of the door. You just carry the violin."

"How're we getting back to the hotel without a car?" Aaron asked.

I wasn't ready for that question. I had been so intent on getting into the hidden room and finding the violin, I had completely forgotten that Benny had taken away Aaron's car keys. Even if we escaped the house, we were stranded out there on La Paloma Road.

"Shit, that's right. We can't exactly call a cab, and it's way too far to walk, even if Sanders and company didn't come after us, which they no doubt will."

We both were silent for a few seconds until Aaron

said in a dejected tone, "I wish one of us had our cell phone…"

Cell phone. Of course. How stupid of me.

"Quick," I said, handing Aaron the flashlight, "shine this on my wrist."

"On your wrist? What…"

"Don't argue. Just do it."

I'd completely forgotten about my fancy new watch. Although I'd bought it for a completely different purpose, I was sure—well, I fervently hoped—it was even more valuable than I'd thought.

"This little baby is more than just a pretty face," I explained to Aaron. "It's one of those high-tech computer watches—you know, a 'smart watch.' I bought the best one they had, of course—my boss was paying for it—and I'll bet it has a phone function…"

I spent a few precious minutes finding it, but sure enough, a phone screen eventually flashed on. We were in business.

****

"Talk about well-prepared. Have you got a Swiss Army knife in there too? You could've been a Boy Scout!" Then, looking at my chest where the lock picks had been concealed, he added, "Maybe not. So do you think if you could get hold of Sara, there's any way she could come and get us?"

I was thinking along the same lines. About the last thing I wanted to do was to ask Sara to come to my rescue, or to involve her directly in our burglary in any way, but I didn't see any alternative. This was indeed the last thing I could do.

"I'd rather not ask her," I said to Aaron, "but there really isn't anyone else we can rely on. Of course, it'd take her at least an hour to get here, so we'll have to avoid capture for that long."

"Ah, that's where my prison escape training comes in," Aaron said.

I was astonished. "You escaped from a prison?"

"Well, no, but I'm a real fan of those prison escape movies, especially the ones where the Americans escape from a Nazi P.O.W. camp, so I know all the techniques."

I couldn't tell in the dark whether Aaron was serious or just trying to lighten the mood. I assumed the latter and smiled, then turned to my wrist and dialed.

****

"Sara?"

"Flo? Are you on the way back? Have you got the violin?"

"Uh, sort of, and yes."

"What's that mean?"

"Yes, we have the violin. We're sort of on our way back, but we've run into a slight problem and need your help." I could almost see Sara's features fall, and the sound of dread in my friend's voice confirmed it.

"You're not gonna ask me to come down there and rescue you, are you? Tell me this time I can stay out of the dangerous parts."

I sighed. I understood perfectly. I wouldn't blame Sara if she hung up before I could ask. But I soldiered on hurriedly.

"I know it's a lot to ask, but Aaron and I were caught and locked in the gallery, and we managed to get into the hidden room next to it where we found Aaron's violin. But Benny took away Aaron's car keys, so we have no way to get back even if we escape the house and grounds. We need you to come down and get us."

"To the Sanders house? You want me to walk into the lion's den and join you there?"

"No, no. We'll get outta here somehow, but we'll need a ride home."

There was silence on the phone, and for a few seconds I thought Sara had indeed hung up. But then a very reluctant voice came back on and asked, "Okay, where do you want me to pick you up?"

"The only place I can think of where we can hide until you get here, and that you'll know how to find, is that little park we used for reconnaissance. Do you think you can find it again?"

"I'll find it. I can use the GPS."

"Can you leave right now?"

"Well, I'm down at the bar in the hotel. I just have to go upstairs to our room and get my keys and stuff. I don't know what traffic will be like. I'll do the best I can."

"Thanks, Sara. We'll make it up to you."

"Yeah. Tell Aaron he owes me big time." Despite the words, I could tell Sara was smiling. She was a trooper, if a reluctant one.

I conveyed the plan to Aaron and then proceeded to examine the outside door. As with the door to the gallery, whoever had built it had seen no reason to conceal the hardware or make it difficult to open from that side, although it probably was securely locked from the outside. A turn of a simple deadbolt was all that was required, and a few minutes later Aaron and I, in an impromptu and unrehearsed remake of "Stalag 17," began our escape.

Chapter 36

I assumed Sara was carrying out her end of the rescue with all due speed—an assumption that proved to be premature, but more on that later—while back at Chez Sanders things were not running as smoothly as they might. Although there had been no problem in getting the outside door to the workshop open, there definitely was a problem leaving the building through it. The door was in full view of the detached garage, where Benny was either taking out a transmission or putting one in; in either case, he was doing it out in front, where he was bound to see us if we attempted to leave through the door. But as there was no other practical way to leave, Aaron and I had to wait until Benny either finished the job or he got tired and went back to the house. We had no idea how long either might take.

A half hour passed. Then an hour. I was sure Marianne would come back to the gallery at any minute and find us missing.

We were still trapped in the workshop watching Benny when my watch/phone vibrated and buzzed softly.

"Sara?"

"Yes. We're here. Where are you?"

"We're still at the house. And who is 'we'?"

"I'll explain later. Why aren't you here yet?"

"Benny, Sanders' driver, is working on a car out in the garage, right where we have to pass. I don't know how long he'll be there."

"Well, can't you get past him somehow?"

"I don't think so, not without taking quite a chance."

"Hmm. So you need to get him away from the garage."

A pause while both sides considered this. At my end, a whispered conversation with Aaron. Then: "How about if you call the house and ask for Benny. He gets called in, and we scoot past while he's away."

"Do you know the number?"

"No, but you probably can find it on the internet using your phone. That's how I found it to call this morning."

"What if there's a phone in the garage?"

I thought about this. "It's possible, but it's worth a try. Even if there is one, it may be far enough inside that we can still sneak past. We'll have to chance it. The longer we wait, the more likely Sanders will come home or Marianne the housekeeper will find us missing from where they locked us up."

Another pause. "Okay. I'll phone as soon as I find the number. Watch to see if he leaves. And good luck."

"Thanks."

I told Aaron the plan. And we waited and watched.

****

Aaron and I waited impatiently for several minutes, watching Benny from a slightly opened door. We strained to hear some kind of ringing sound to indicate that Sara had found the number and called, but as we were at least two rooms away from where the nearest phone might be, we heard nothing. Nevertheless, after about five minutes had passed we saw Benny put down his tools and trudge slowly from the garage across the gravel driveway and toward the house.

We knew we had only a minute or two between the time Benny took the phone and the point at which whatever ruse Sara had used to get him there became ineffective. As soon as Benny disappeared behind the side of the house, I opened the door and motioned Aaron to follow me. He had wrapped the red velvet blanket around the instrument to protect it, and he carried it as gingerly as if it were a bottle of nitro-glycerin, precisely like a person trying to avoid a second violin-crushing incident in one day.

We closed the door, which opened inward, as far as we could, then half-ran to the corner of the building, where I peeked around to see if the coast was still clear. It was, and we scooted across the open space of the circular driveway, keeping low just in case Benny or Marianne happened to glance out the front window just at that inopportune moment. Across the driveway we took refuge in the thick privet hedge lining the drive.

So far so good.

Concealed from the house by the hedge, we began to inch our way down the drive toward the security gate. It was after five o'clock and I hoped Jerry had already ended his shift and gone home.

We had not gone more than ten feet when we heard the front door of the house slam and Benny trudge back across the gravel, back to the garage. We froze. He was unlikely to notice us anyway, however, because from the way his feet were pounding the ground with every step and he was muttering loudly, it was obvious he was more than a little pissed off at being called away for Sara's bogus phone call.

Once Benny was back at work in the garage, Aaron and I proceeded down the side of the drive, still hidden by the privet hedge. When we finally arrived at the security gate, it didn't seem to be manned, by Jerry or anyone else. We were both letting out a sigh of relief, Aaron even flashing me the thumbs-up sign, when we heard about the last sound we wanted to hear just then: the soft whine of a car's motor as a Prius with the livery of a Yellow Cab climbed slowly up the drive, no doubt carrying James Edward Sanders, grocery store magnate, collector of illicit art, and soon-to-be extremely irritated employer.

****

I wondered whether Marianne had actually gotten hold of Sanders or she was just trying to put a scare into us. On the other hand, it didn't really matter, because if he didn't know about us already, he would very soon, including the fact that the would-be burglars were no longer imprisoned in the gallery. I hoped it would take a little longer to discover that we had escaped through the workshop, and that we had taken the Guarneri with us. Because at that point, the excrement would absolutely hit the whirling blades of the Sanders fan.

When the cab came to an abrupt halt just on the other side of the hedge, I almost fainted. If Sanders had spotted us, our chances of making it to the rendezvous with Sara were sharply reduced. My hand grasped Aaron's tightly as we waited to see whether we should try to run for it. But if we did try, the fact that Aaron was carrying a very vulnerable treasure would be sure to slow us down.

We breathed easier when we peeked out and saw that the cab had stopped only for the security gate to be opened, and once it was the Prius continued on its way to the house. As soon as it was out of sight, we continued down the drive until we finally came out on La Paloma Road.

A few minutes later we were across the road and walking up the drive to Little Hyde Park.

Chapter 37

As soon as we entered the parking lot of the park, I looked around for Sara's white BMW. But the only car there was a dark red Chrysler with two people in it. I was about to call Sara to find out where the hell she was when my friend emerged from the passenger side of the Chrysler and ran toward me and Aaron. I was confused as to how Sara had gotten there, but I definitely was glad to see her, whether she had arrived in a Chrysler, a BMW, or a 747.

After a quick exchange of hugs, Sara briefly explained why she had had to borrow both a car and a driver for this rescue mission. I got the rest of the story later, of course, and it went something like this:

Apparently the previous evening, while Aaron and I were playing Mr. and Mrs., she had been out with her new friend Roger, he of the luxurious suite in the Mark Hopkins. They had used our car, the BMW, and Sara was so tired when she got back and parked it, she had left the lights on. So when she tried to start it after our phone call, the battery was dead.

There was no time to find a car rental agency and rent another car. Nor was there time to get the BMW's battery charged or replaced. Finding a cab could also take time, especially one willing to take her to Los Altos. So she phoned Roger and pleaded with him to lend her his car, explaining that it was an emergency, "a matter of life and death." He said he was sorry but he couldn't do that, and besides she sounded too panicky to drive safely. So he offered to drive her wherever she needed to go. What a guy! (Of course, I'm sure Sara said she would make it up to him, and I'm sure Roger hoped so, but that was no time to question his motives.)

Once they were on the highway headed for Los Altos, Roger could tell Sara was a bundle of nerves, and naturally he wanted to know what kind of emergency mission they were on.

"Hey, relax. It can't be that serious," he said to Sara. "I mean, if it were a medical emergency, I'm sure your friend would've called a doctor or ambulance, not you. And if it was some kind of criminal threat, she would've called 911."

Sara didn't respond, so Roger tried again:

"Uh, could you give me a hint just what kind of trouble it is that your friend is in?"

Sara said she thought this over. Roger was bound to find out once they had rescued Aaron and me. But if she told him then, she was afraid he might turn around and go back. She decided to chance it.

"Well, I'll tell you if you promise you'll still take me there," she told Roger.

Roger's eyebrows went up a bit, but otherwise he didn't display any alarm.

"Okay, I promise. But I don't guarantee I'll get involved in whatever it is."

So Sara went ahead and told him the truth, a commodity in somewhat short supply on this mission. "Well, I'm not sure…that is…anyway, I've got this friend, Flo. She makes her living by…well…by taking things. From people's homes."

This time Roger's eyebrows almost reached his hairline. "You mean she's a burglar?"

"That's right."

"And you're one too?" He looked over at Sara and almost swerved off the road.

"No, of course not. I'm just her friend. But sometimes friends are called on to help friends in situations where friendship is more important than the legal technicalities, if you know what I mean."

Apparently it was not clear Roger did know, but all he said was, "I see. And is this 'mission' we're on one of those…'situations'?"

"Yes. I mean no, not exactly. Oh, it's complicated." And so she proceeded to tell him the whole story, from Aaron's previously-stolen violin to our attempt to steal it back, with two murders in between. When she was finished, and they were only a few miles from Los Altos, Roger was silent for a while. He seemed to be thinking it all over, and Sara says she was sure he was going to refuse to take her any farther. When he spoke, his tone was serious.

"You know, bastards like this guy Sanders get away with all kinds of shit because they can't be touched. They've got money, they've got influence, and they've got power. And while I can't say I approve of your friend's profession in general, what she's doing now seems like just what the sonofabitch deserves. And I'll be glad to help her do it."

Sara leaned over and kissed Roger on the cheek. He smiled and they drove the rest of the way in silence.

And that's why it was Roger's Chrysler, with Roger at the wheel, that showed up at Little Hyde Park.

Chapter 38

Needless to say, I was seldom so glad to see my friend Sara as I was when she got out of Roger's Chrysler. As for how and why, I wasn't sure I'd caught all of the nuances, but I got the drift of what Sara was telling me and assured her we would be honored to be rescued by both Sara and her current partner. Even if I'd been concerned about a stranger learning about my criminal activities, I was in no position to express it.

Although there was no time to waste, both Aaron and I had gone a long time without a bathroom break, and there were two rest rooms beckoning to us just yards behind where Roger had parked. I for one simply couldn't wait for our next chance, and I imagined Aaron was in a similar condition. We quickly excused ourselves and ran for the privies, Aaron first laying the velvet-wrapped violin carefully down on a nearby picnic table and telling Sara to keep her eye on it. Seeing that there would be a delay anyway, Roger got out of the car and ducked into the men's room after Aaron. Sara apparently had had the sense to go before leaving town, so she stayed to stand guard.

In retrospect, this was another dumb move, and all three of us should've just wet our pants. Perhaps a minute after we entered the rest rooms, the Sanders Mercedes sped up the driveway of the park and came to a screeching halt in back of Roger's car. Benny leaped out of the driver's door and approached Sara, who was standing alone next to the Chrysler. Sara, having recognized the Sanders Mercedes from our reconnaissance, tried to run away, which Benny, who despite his appearance wasn't incapable of putting two and two together and getting four, correctly interpreted as guilt. Before she could escape, Benny caught her by the arm.

Sara started to scream, but Benny put a huge hand over her mouth. "Well, well," he said in a loud, menacing voice. "I was just lookin' for someone who might've seen a coupla strangers runnin' down the road, and look what I found instead. I'll bet you're waitin' for them now. Well, we'll just wait together."

Sara struggled to break free, but Benny was much too strong for her.

"Settle down now," he growled, "or they'll be takin' you home feet first. And you're much too pretty for that."

During most of this action, Aaron, Roger, and I were watching and listening from the rest room doors, which were only a few feet behind Benny's back. None of us knew exactly how to respond. But as soon as Sara's life seemed to be in jeopardy, inaction was no longer an option. I was the first to start toward Benny, the sound of my movements masked by the wind in the surrounding trees. But before I could take two steps from the rest room door I was grabbed by a strong hand and pulled back. Roger motioned me to stay there and be quiet.

Roger had taken off his shoes so as to make no sound as he crept up behind Benny. He had something in his hand. In the fading light Aaron and I couldn't see exactly what was taking place, but a few seconds later Benny had let Sara go and was lying face down on the ground, while Sara ran to join Aaron and me.

As I soon learned, what Roger was carrying was a small-caliber pistol; and what he said to Benny was, in effect, that he could let Sara go or he would be the one leaving the park feet first. Benny chose the former, after which Roger ordered him down on the ground.

"Sara, move this guy's car away from behind ours, will you?" Roger said.

But Sara was too shaken to drive even a few yards, so Aaron did the honors instead. He hustled over to the Mercedes, which was still running, and parked it at the end of the lot. He got out and threw the keys into the underbrush, a little impromptu touch that I had to admire. Then with Benny still lying on the ground, Sara, Aaron, and I got into the Chrysler. Roger, still holding his gun on Benny, backed up to the men's room door, where he slipped back into his loafers, said something threatening to Benny that I didn't quite catch, and while keeping an eye and his gun on the prostrate figure on the ground, got behind the wheel of his car. He pulled the door shut and with squealing tires the Chrysler headed for the parking lot exit.

Benny got up from the ground.

Before the Chrysler got to the exit, however, it came to a screeching stop, and then quickly reversed direction and retraced its path, stopping abruptly just in front of the rest rooms. The rear passenger door flew open, and Aaron leapt out, a frantic look on his face. Benny, having already had more than he bargained for with these crazy people, took off running. But Aaron wasn't chasing Benny. Instead, he ran straight to the picnic table where he had left his Guarneri. He grabbed it and its velvet cover, hugged them to his chest, and dashed back into the car, slamming the door well after the car was already moving at speed back toward the exit.

Just how embarrassing would it have been, after all we had been through, to have left the prize behind on a picnic table?

Words could not have described it.

Chapter 39

The drive home was relatively uneventful, considering the circumstances. We stopped at the Terrace Inn to pay the bill and collect "Mr. and Mrs. Levy's" luggage, then headed north. On the way we gave Sara and Roger a brief outline of our adventures in Chez Sanders.

After that, we were all silent, thinking our own thoughts, until I said, "So, Roger. We're really very grateful for your help, but did Sara tell you what we were doing down there and why we needed to be rescued?" Remember, I hadn't yet gotten the full story from Sara, and I wouldn't until later that evening.

"She did," he said. "And at first it sounded like she was asking me to help you make a getaway from a burglary."

"And you came anyway?"

"Well, when I heard the whole story I realized that I'd be helping the good guys, not the bad guys. And it sounded like an adventure. I love adventures." He looked back at me and smiled. I could see why Sara had been attracted to him.

Aaron said that he personally was less enamored of adventures than he had been a few days earlier.

Sara then took her turn at questioning Roger. "You didn't tell me you were carrying that gun. In fact, you told me you were the CEO of a big company. Do

CEO's always 'pack heat'?"

Roger laughed. "Well, no. But the kind of business we do has certain…certain personal risks attached to it. I find it prudent to carry a means of self-protection."

"I assume you have a permit for that thing?" Aaron asked.

"Oh sure. It's all legal. And don't think I'm one of these gun nuts who carries a weapon as some sort of macho statement. I hate having to carry it, but I've learned to live with it."

"I'll bet you never expected to be using it quite this way," I said.

Roger shook his head slowly.

"Not in a million years."

****

A few minutes of silence later, I said to no one in particular, "I wonder whether Sanders has discovered that his violin is missing—"

"My violin," Aaron corrected me.

I smiled. "Excuse me, whether Aaron's violin is missing?"

"Even if he's discovered it, and he wants to come after us, he doesn't have any idea who we are or where we're headed," Sara said.

"Unless that muscle-head who attacked you got my license number, I suppose," Roger said.

"That seems unlikely," Sara said. "And besides, what would they do with the number if they had it? Even if they were able to trace your car, we're not talking about the Mafia here, but a rich guy who collects stolen art. He might try to steal the violin back if you had it, but you don't."

"No," Aaron said, "I'll have it. And Sanders is

probably smart enough to figure that out. And when he does, even if technically we broke the law, he certainly won't call in the police. I mean, I assume it's generally frowned upon for a thief to enlist the aid of the law in recovering his loot from the person he stole it from. 'Excuse me, officer, but that man just stole his own violin from me.' And then there's the fact his employee murdered Donny Martin. I'm sure Sanders wants no part of the police."

"What if he does try to steal it back again?" I asked.

"Don't worry. I'm not going to be that stupid a second time. I won't be traveling with the violin any more. When I use it on tour, it will be in the hands of a security company, and they'll keep it safe in transit. And of course I won't be keeping it in my hotel room, like the copy." He gave me a wink.

We all agreed that Sanders would not be bothering us that evening, at least. There were, however, several matters still to be sorted out among the car's passengers.

Roger said, "Tell me, Aaron, was this a typical episode in the life of a concert violinist?"

Aaron laughed. "Well, let me see. For about the last thirty years, my normal routine has consisted of hours and hours of practice each day, and days and days of travel each month. About the most exciting things I've done are to walk in the park or make a quick trip back to Israel to see my parents, so my mother can tell me how tired I look and ask why don't I eat more vegetables. Whereas in the last few weeks I've…"— and here he ticked off each point on his fingers— "…had my violin stolen by a very bad person, caught a very pretty burglar…"—he glanced over at me, and I'm pretty sure I blushed slightly—"…and with her equally gorgeous friend…"—Sara's turn to blush—"…planned my own burglary, discovered a murder, been stalked by a starry-eyed young woman, pretended to be gay, burglarized someone's house, driven a getaway car, been locked in an art gallery, had terrific sex, been—"

"Hold on there," Sara interrupted, turning to face Aaron. "What's this sex thing?"

"Never mind!" I said as I put my hand on Aaron's chest to indicate he had said enough. "He's just trying to be funny. And I think he's trying too hard."

This last was directed at Aaron, who got the message, because he concluded his answer to Roger quickly with, "So as you can see, just same old same old."

"Hmmm," was all Sara replied, but she let the matter drop.

****

A few miles later, Aaron said in a sober tone, "You know, it's great having my violin back, of course, but for all the risks we took, we didn't end up getting hold of the gun that killed Donny Martin. We know who did it, Marianne, and she admitted it was with her deadly little pistol, but it's her word against ours. Flo is still facing a possible murder charge."

"Not necessarily," I said to him. "Listen."

I tapped a few times on my fancy new watch—the one Marianne didn't think worth taking away—and there, loud and clear was Marianne, retelling the story of how she murdered Martin.

Aaron was clearly impressed, from the fact his mouth was momentarily hanging open.

"My God, Flo, is there anything that watch can't do?" He told Sara how we'd managed to call her without a cell phone. To me he said, "Bringing that was pure genius."

"Maybe not genius," I said, "but I told you how important good planning was. I knew there might be challenges on this job for which a few burglar tools wouldn't suffice, so I decided I'd go high-tech and bought myself this neat little smartwatch, something I've wanted but could never afford on my own. But with your money…. Anyway, I'm sure Marianne's confession will be all I need to avoid the electric chair, or whatever it is they use these days."

Sara clapped her hands. Aaron put his arm around me and gave me a kiss, saying, "Best present I ever bought anyone, and I didn't even know I was buying it."

Next it was Roger's turn. "So Sara's told me most of the story," he said, "and I now understand the housekeeper-cum-concubine/hit woman killed this fellow Martin. But I'm not sure I'm clear on who shot the other fellow. The roommate."

There was no response until I finally piped up, "I really don't know who shot Martin's roommate, Ballard. Marianne denied it was her, and there was no reason for her to lie, as she freely admitted to killing Martin. If it was one of Sanders' men, that would point to Aaron's friend Rafael, who was the go-between sent to pay Ballard and collect the violin. But from what Aaron has said about Rafael, and the fact the money was still in Ballard's wallet, it just doesn't seem likely he was the killer." Aaron nodded agreement. "But then, Marianne didn't seem like one at first, either. And if it wasn't Rafael, who else could it have been?"

There was a long silence. Then Aaron spoke, almost inaudibly:

"Me."

****

Needless to say, there was what is commonly known as a stunned silence. We all looked at Aaron, Roger in the rearview mirror so that he nearly ran off the road. He quickly found a place to turn off and parked by the side of the road "so I don't miss any of this."

I asked the obvious question: "What do you mean, 'me'? I mean you?"

Aaron, looking somewhat sheepish, cleared his throat and said, "I mean I killed Fred Ballard. Or at least I was responsible for it. I didn't mean to, but still…"

"Wait!" I shouted over the passing traffic noise. "Please start at the beginning."

"Sure. Well, you remember I told you that, according to Rafael, Ballard said he had the violin, but it would be a couple of days before he could give it to Sanders and get his 'reward'?"

"Yes."

"Well, I got this crazy idea. I'd get to Ballard first, while he still had the violin, and offer him twice what Sanders was paying for the violin. In cash. He could just disappear and when Rafael showed up with the money, he'd be gone and twice as wealthy. Rafael would report back to Sanders that when he got to Ballard's place, he wasn't there."

Sara whistled and said, "It was worth that much to you?"

"Yeah, it was. I knew stealing it back was both dangerous and chancy. Rafael had told me how much Sanders was paying for it, and to me it was well worth twice that to get it back with no risk, either of harm or failure."

"Okay," I said, "but we know Sanders ended up with the violin and Ballard ended up dead. So what happened?"

"Well, Rafael told me where Ballard was staying, which was in Redwood City, not far from Los Altos. So I told you I had business to attend to and I caught a flight to San Francisco. But the plane was delayed, and by the time I arrived it was the middle of the night and I had to wait until the next morning to drive to Redwood City. But when I finally got there and found Ballard, it was too late. Sanders had arrived back earlier than expected, and the exchange had already been made."

"So obviously you didn't shoot Ballard to get the violin," I said.

Aaron turned and gave me a rather severe look. "Of course not!" he said. "How could you even suggest such a thing?"

"Sorry. I'm just trying to follow the story. If the violin was already gone, why did you shoot Ballard?"

"I didn't shoot him. Well, yes, I did, but not like you're thinking. Let me finish the story."

I shut up and put my finger across my lips.

"When I found out the violin was gone, I said something like 'Thanks, anyway,' and started to leave. But Ballard was, of course, not a businessman, but a hardened criminal. I should have suspected he would realize that, thinking he still had the violin, I came there carrying a shitload of cash to pay for it. He decided he wanted to relieve me of that considerable amount of money, and he took out a gun from a holster under his arm and told me to put the cash on the table in front of me."

"Jesus," I said.

"Right. So now I'll remind you that, as an Israeli citizen, following university I spent two years in the Israeli army. I was trained in, among other gentle pastimes, hand-to-hand combat. It was almost too easy to disarm Ballard, but the gun fell to the floor and Ballard dove after it."

Sara almost squealed. "God, this is like a real-life movie."

Aaron smiled, then finished his story. "I went after it too, and in the ensuing struggle, the gun went off and killed Ballard. A useful tip: If you're ever fighting over a loaded gun, even if you can't fully get hold of it, always try to make sure the barrel is pointed toward the other guy."

No one spoke for at least thirty seconds as we absorbed what Aaron had said. I broke the silence.

"So you were that close to...to not coming back with us." I didn't know whether I wanted to laugh or cry. I decided just to give Aaron a hug.

"I guess so," he said. "And it would've been my own fault. I should've figured a crook like Ballard would try to hold me up, knowing I was carrying so much cash. So I was lucky to get away with it."

Suddenly something occurred to me. "Just a minute," I said. "Why didn't you just take the gun away from Marianne when she was holding it on us? Too chivalrous to hit a lady?"

Aaron laughed. "Maybe. No, it was because, first

of all, Benny was there and armed, so the odds weren't very good. And you were there, and I wouldn't have risked your getting hurt in whatever melee followed."

"Hmm, okay," I said. "That sounds plausible."

"One other thing," Sara said. "That article in the newspaper said they didn't find the gun that killed Ballard. What happened to it?"

"Oh, I've still got it. I took it because I thought at the time it might be the gun that killed Martin. I wrapped it in a handkerchief like I see the cops do on TV to preserve Ballard's fingerprints on it. But of course we now know that Marianne killed Martin, not Ballard."

"So what will you do with the gun now?" Roger asked.

"Throw it in San Francisco Bay as soon as we get back to the city. I sure don't want it. And I sure don't want it found on me. As far as I can tell, nothing else connects me with Ballard or his death, and I want to keep it that way—an unsolved mystery."

"And only we know the solution to the mystery," Sara said, clapping her hands. "How neat."

Okay, so if you're reading this, now you know, too.

Chapter 40

When we arrived back at the Fairmont, Roger dropped me and Aaron off, then asked Sara if she'd like to come over to the Mark Hopkins with him for a drink. "These two must be pretty tired," he said, "so they won't be any fun tonight."

Sara probably was tempted, but she declined. "To tell the truth," she said, "I can't wait to hear what happened down there. Obviously things didn't go the way Flo planned, or we wouldn't have had to come to their rescue."

Roger nodded. "I understand. Maybe tomorrow? Then you can tell me what happened too. At least the unclassified parts."

"Would you like to come along now and listen?" Sara asked. It wasn't a good idea, but she probably felt obligated to offer.

Roger waved the idea away. "No, thanks. I'd just be intruding. I'm sure you three have lots to talk about, and some of it probably shouldn't go any farther. I'm just a stranger who was available to help out."

Sara leaned over and kissed Roger affectionately on the cheek. "You're not a stranger anymore, but I guess you're right. I'll see you tomorrow. Maybe we can all have that drink together."

Aaron and I joined in agreement at this plan, and our little band of conspirators got out of the car. Aaron, still treating his violin like a newborn baby, thanked Roger again, and we walked up the steps and into the hotel.

We headed straight for the elevators, but on the way we stopped at the concierge desk, where Aaron asked the clerk, "Is this where I bring something to have it put in the hotel safe?"

"Yes, sir," the clerk said. "And there's no charge for that service."

"Good. I'll want this violin put in the safe as soon as I get the case from my room."

"Very wise, sir," the clerk commented as Aaron departed for his room. "You'd be surprised the valuable things some of our guests have left in their hotel rooms, just asking for them to be stolen."

Aaron nodded in agreement, then directed a wink in my direction. "Someday they might just walk into their room and find a burglar there.

"No telling what might happen then."

****

It was nine o'clock in the evening. Aaron, Sara and I had showered and changed in our respective suites, and we had all gathered in Aaron's for the debriefing. Aaron sat on a loveseat, across from us girls, who sat next to each other on a sofa. On the coffee table between us was an open bottle of champagne, and each of us held a partially-filled glass of bubbly.

This was not simply a chance to satisfy Sara's understandable curiosity about what had gone wrong— and what had gone right—at Chez Sanders, as well as get the full story behind Roger's appearance in the cast of characters, but also a necessary opportunity for me to assess, in a less stressful, more relaxed setting, just why

Aaron and I had found ourselves in such dire straits. Was it all because of my clumsiness with the fake violin? Was it also poor planning? Should I have anticipated the gallery being off limits? What if it had been the real Guarneri that got crushed when I fell on it? Maybe everything turned out for the best.

Sara sat spellbound as I related the details of our exploits in the Sanders house, at first seemingly successful but ending with the wrong violin, then seemingly unsuccessful but ending with the right one. Sara asked an occasional question, and Aaron inserted an occasional detail, but mostly I told the whole story.

Well, perhaps not the whole story, if one considers my omission of the details of our little episode in the Terrace Inn. But from Sara's expression as I told this part of the story, her eyebrows arching and eyes widening tellingly, it was unlikely she was fooled by my sanitized version of the facts, especially after Aaron's unfortunate statement in the car. And face it, Sara is hardly a stranger to impromptu sexual encounters herself.

When I had reached the events that included Sara, I stopped.

There was a long silence as Sara digested the details.

"Whew," she said at last, "I'm sure that was about as close as you ever want to come to getting caught."

"Absolutely," I said.

"And as for me," Aaron added, "that was enough of a crime spree to last me a lifetime. From now on I don't even intend to risk jaywalking."

Sara laughed. "That's what I always say after getting involved in one of Flo's little capers; but I always seem to come back for more when I'm called. I guess I'm either spineless and can't say no, or I'm a glutton for punishment."

I leaned over and kissed Sara on the cheek. "No, you're just a wonderful friend who wouldn't stand by and let me drown if she could save me."

Sara took my hand and squeezed it.

"Hey," Aaron protested, "don't I get a little love here too? I was the one who pushed Flo in, remember. She didn't even want to go swimming with me. Turns out she was right."

As one, Sara and I got up and crossed over to where Aaron was sitting. We sat down on either side of him and kissed him on both cheeks simultaneously. He in turn put his arms around our waists, and we sat together in silence for at least a minute before Aaron turned to me and asked, "While we're explaining things, how about telling me how you opened that lock? I've always wondered about that."

"Me too," Sara added. "What's the secret?"

"It's no secret. You just have to understand how a lock works. That's what I learned in the locksmith course I took. It's a little hard to explain."

"So give us the simplified version," Sara said.

I did my best to explain, in a few words, about tumblers and pins and cylinders and how a lock pick imitates a key.

"Sounds pretty difficult to me," Aaron said when I was finished.

"It just takes a lot of practice," I said.

Aaron took my hand and said, "Do you think we could schedule a private lesson or two when I'm next in Seattle?"

"Absolutely," I said. I'd been hoping our extracurricular encounter was more than just a temporary testosterone rush on Aaron's part.

"Which reminds me," Aaron continued, "that I haven't practiced my violin in several days now, having spent entirely too much time playing cops and robbers. Well, robbers, anyway."

Sara, who had been leaning back and had begun daydreaming a bit about locks and violins and Roger, suddenly sat straight up and said, "Wait a minute. I just thought of something. Didn't you have a car when you left here, a rented car? Where is it?"

Somehow in the euphoria of the violin recovery and our successful escape, we had all forgotten about the Chevrolet in which Aaron and I had driven down to Chez Sanders. And left there, the keys having been confiscated by Benny.

I was having visions of yet another foray to the Sanders estate, this one to steal a car. It was not a pleasant prospect. In fact, it was more like a nightmare.

"Okay," I said, "let's not panic. They've got the rental car. I see at least two problems. First, we have to explain that to the rental people and somehow get it back to them. And second, what will having the car tell Sanders about who took his violin?"

"MY violin," Aaron corrected me again. He didn't sound worried. "And what it will tell him is that I took it. You'll be in the clear, of course, because the rental contract papers in the glove compartment have only my name on them. So he'll know the person who 'stole' his violin is the same person from whom he stole it first."

"So is that bad?" Sara asked. "I mean, he might've figured out who took it anyway, or recognized you from the description Benny and Marianne would've given him."

"Actually, I don't know that it's either good or bad," Aaron said. "That is, even if he knows for sure I took my violin back, like we agreed earlier, what's he gonna do about it? He can't call the police, and he can't sue me." He paused. "Well, technically, I suppose he can sue me for trespass or something, but I can't imagine he'd want it coming out in the trial that he traffics in stolen artwork. No, I think he'll be smart enough to concede this round to me."

"But there's still the matter of the rental car itself," I said. "What do we tell the company? That it got impounded while we were committing a burglary?"

Aaron laughed. "No, I don't think so. I think we'll tell them it broke down while we were visiting friends in Los Altos, and it was too late at night to try to get it towed, so it's still there, and we'll be glad to pay to have it towed back to San Francisco, or some closer place if possible. It might even be covered by that insurance I purchased with it."

"And what happens when they try to get it from Sanders?" Sara asked.

"Well, let's see. He might deny he has it, in which case we'll say it must've been stolen, from where we left it. Then he's stuck with it, because he can't sell it if it's hot. Or he might say it was left by burglars who got away, but that incriminates me and drops him right into the same public mess as if he'd called the police on us. No, I think he'll let them come and get it. And worst case scenario, I end up having to pay for the damn thing. Not what I want to do, but it's still cheap considering the value of my violin. Not to mention the adventure that came with it."

"So all in all," Sara said to Aaron, "I take it you would consider your first burglary—"

"First and only," Aaron inserted.

"…your first and only burglary to have been a success."

"I would." He lifted his champagne glass and said to me and Sara, "To the beginning and end of my life of crime. And to the continued success of yours."

That seemed to satisfy everyone, and when the champagne was gone, we called it a day. A day, a night, a week, and a job.

A job with more than a few strings attached.

Thank you for purchasing
this publication of The Wild Rose Press, Inc.

For questions or more information
contact us at
info@thewildrosepress.com.

The Wild Rose Press, Inc.
www.thewildrosepress.com

CPSIA information can be obtained
at www.ICGtesting.com
Printed in the USA
LVHW050203100321
680971LV00002B/60

9 781509 233212